Ark Two

TOM SWIFT®
ARK TWO
VICTOR APPLETON

WANDERER BOOKS
Published by Simon & Schuster, New York

Published by WANDERER BOOKS
A Simon & Schuster Division of
Gulf & Western Corporation
Simon & Schuster Building
1230 Avenue of the Americas
New York, New York 10020

Manufactured in the United States of America
10 9 8 7 6 5 4 3 2 1

WANDERER and colophon are trademarks of Simon & Schuster

TOM SWIFT is a trademark of Stratemeyer Syndicate, registered in
the United States Patent and Trademark Office

Library of Congress Cataloging in Publication Data
Appleton, Victor, pseud.
Ark two.
(Tom Swift ; no. 7)
Summary: Tom Swift and his crew travel to the planet Aquilla
to recover SeaGlobe, an ecological system stolen from the space
colony New America.
[1. Science fiction]   I. Title. II. Series:
Appleton, Victor, pseud. Tom Swift ; no. 7.
PZ7.A652Ar   81–21890
ISBN 0–671–43952–9   AACR2
ISBN 0–671–43953–7 (pbk.)

CONTENTS

Chapter One

"We have about forty-five minutes before we dock at *New America*," Tom Swift said to his friend Ben Walking Eagle. "If you'll take the wheel, I'd like to test my latest invention." He jerked a thumb at a squat metal square strapped to the deck of their spaceship *Exedra*. Thick plastic cables led from the box to the starboard bulkhead, linking the device to both the power and computer lines of the *Exedra*.

"Sure, buddy. Move over."

Tom snapped himself out of his contoured pilot seat and drifted in the null gravity to the deck, steadying his path with grips built into the hull.

"This should be fun," Anita Thorwald said. "I hope it tests out okay after all the work we put into it." She shook her long, red hair and eyed the box with just the slightest bit of apprehension in her lovely eyes.

Tom, the blond-haired genius of the group, his buddy Ben, who was a computer expert, and Anita had spent months perfecting the shadowlator, which was designed to scramble light waves around a spacecraft and render it virtually invisible to even the most sophisticated detection devices. Tests in Swift Enterprises' Triton dome off the Florida coast had proved promising, and Tom was anxious to operate the device under zero-gravity conditions.

Tom turned to his robot. "Activate, Artistotle. I need your help on this."

The huge mechanoid released his safety brackets and moved away from the wall. "All components clear and ready," he spoke up.

"Thanks." Tom snapped open the shadowlator and switched on its circuits. Amber safety lights blinked. The eighteen-year-old inventor selected multicolored wires from the shadowlator's test board and clipped them to leads on Artistotle's chest. "I've got clear power here," Tom called over his shoulder. "Check your panels, Ben."

"Power steady. You've got a good wave on my scope."

"I'm running a thirty-second transmission test through your monitors," Tom told Artistotle. "Match it against your chips from the lab and let's see what we come up with."

"We *should* get a truer curve out here, Tom, away from atmospheric interference," Aristotle said. "That is the effect we—"

"Right," Tom cut him short. "I'm running a five-second pulse." He ran his fingers over the board, flipping the standby switches to ON.

Suddenly, white light exploded in the small cabin. Tom's safety visor snapped down over his face. A shock wave slammed into his stomach and hurled him toward the rear of the ship. "Ben!" he cried out. "Cut the power—quick!" Ben didn't answer. He was slumped in his seat, dazed.

Alarm bells clanged through the *Exedra*. Tom thrust out his arm to keep from smashing against the wall. From the corner of his eye, he saw Aristotle shudder and then go stiff. Ball lightning raced about the cabin, licking at every surface.

Tom rolled himself into a ball, kicked off the aft bulkhead, and shot forward. Catching himself on the arm of Ben's chair, he threw a gloved hand against the emergency cutoff. Instantly, the crackling display of fireworks came to a halt. Auxiliary lights glowed dimly overhead. Tom flipped back his visor as whirring fans began drawing out the acid smell of burning plastic and metal.

"Ben—you okay?"

"Yeah—guess so . . ."

"Anita?"

The girl blinked, stared anxiously past Tom, and sniffed the air. "What—on earth happened back there?"

"Beats me. All I know is we suddenly got about forty times more power than we needed when I turned on that rig." Tom cast a worried eye at the rear of the cabin. "I'm afraid poor Aristotle got the worst of it. He's welded to the wall—probably fried every microchip in his head."

The young Indian computer tech ran a hand through his black hair and gave Tom a searching look. "If I hadn't gotten a jolt of that power myself, I'd say an overload like that was impossible on the *Exedra*."

"It is," Tom said. "There are enough safeties to shoot the odds of a burnout right off the graph. The only trouble is, it happened."

He pulled himself into his seat and ran a quick check of the *Exedra*'s systems. He had a good idea of what to expect. Nearly every light on the board flashed red. The computer was burned to a crisp—which meant navigation, engineering, and guidance were dead, too.

"We're running blind," Ben said gloomily, flipping one switch after another. "I can't reach any Earth station, or sat-coms, either."

They realized that the only areas working on the *Exedra* were the emergency life support system, the auxiliary lights, and the manual guidance system. The nuclear engines were sealed and self-contained, but their instrumentation was not.

"Looks like we go in by the seat of our pants," Tom agreed.

Both boys were thinking the same thing. With any luck at all, *New America*, the space colony they were headed for, would pick up their emergency signal. The small transmitter was independently powered, and could send out a continual bleep as long as its solar batteries kept functioning. Rescue tugs or a nearby Space Marine patrol would come to their help, and they could avoid the tricky business of matching docking velocity without computer guidance.

If they were lucky.

"You're okay," Ben said, peering intently into a small radarscope he had switched to auxiliary power. "Just stay on this heading. You don't want an intercept yet, do you?"

Tom shook his head firmly. "I don't want one at *all*, unless I have to. I'd rather let those boys spot us and come to the rescue."

"You're thinking the same thing I am, aren't

you?" Ben Walking Eagle's voice showed his concern.

"About the overload?" Tom nodded. "Too much of a coincidence. First we had the blowout in Triton dome, then a fire in the lab that shouldn't have happened. Now this. We—"

Before he could finish, the *Exedra* shuddered and pitched violently to port.

"Two blips!" Ben shouted. "Fast across our bow!"

Tom yanked the *Exedra* into a spine-twisting outside loop. He glanced out the starboard glassite port in time to see two blinking sheets of red sizzle past the hull. "Lasers!" His throat tightened. "Would you believe 'accident' number four?"

"If one of those hits us, it'll slice the *Exedra* in half," yelled Ben. "Tom—hard a'port!"

Tom wrenched the ship sharply about. Deadly beams whipped across the bow where the craft had been a split-second before. He caught a quick glimpse of two dark shapes against the stars. Their unfamiliar silhouettes raised the hairs on the back of his neck. The ships were black and ugly, each topped with a dozen sharp spines, like the rays of some deep-water fish.

The two strange vessels were tracking them with computers. Speed, angle of attack, and weapons control were operating together seemingly with one objective in mind: destroy the *Exedra*. Tom, on the other hand, was flying nearly blind. The dark enemy craft knew exactly where he was going, and how long it would take him to get there. He couldn't win. The lasers would miss them once, maybe twice. Then—

Ben gripped the arm of his chair, his features tense. "Coming in fast . . ." he called out over his shoulder. "Two o'clock . . . forty degrees high. Tom," he added as calmly as he could, "I suggest we do something—right *now* would be fine."

"What'd you have in mind, old buddy?"

"How do I know? You're the boss!"

Tom held his course, forcing himself to keep the *Exedra* steady though every instinct told him to veer off and run. The wrong thing at the wrong time was their only chance now. The enemy computers knew exactly when he was supposed to change course, jerk the *Exedra* aside. Their microchip components were solving the problem at light-splitting speeds, faster than any human mind could imagine.

The black vessels came straight for the *Exedra*. Tom feinted left, right, left again, then jerked out of his zigzag course and headed for the enemy ships.

Red lights flashed inches off to port. Another deadly beam laced a thin scar down the *Exedra*'s hull. Thunder shook the small vessel as the raiders sheered off from a near collision course. Tom pulled back the wheel and stood the *Exedra* on its tail, throwing all the power he could muster into the engines. The ship howled, hurtling itself like a comet across the dark fabric of space.

"Close, friend." Ben swallowed hard.

"Too close," Tom agreed. "That won't work more than once, and they know it, too. Where are they?"

Ben squinted into the scope, but realized that it was useless with weakened power. Tom brought the nose up, offering Ben a view through the cabin's overhead port.

"Far to starboard, about ten degrees," Ben reported. A low whistle escaped his lips. "I thought the *Exedra* was fast, but those boys have us beat from here to Christmas." His forehead creased in thought. "If you can't beat 'em, confuse 'em to death, right?"

Tom nodded.

"I know what you're doing. And you're correct up to a point. The computers on those vessels are based on logic, just like ours. Your random maneuver worked fine. But next time, you'll be feeding chance factors into their hopper, giving 'em more to work with."

"I don't care about making a career out of this," Tom groaned. "If I can get away with it a couple more times I'll be happy."

"A *couple* is about all you'll get," warned Ben. He craned his neck upwards, peering into the starry blackness of space. Red lights from the panel flashed off his coppery skin. "They're still coming!" He yanked the radar extension around before him. "*New America* is over the horizon," he said anxiously. "You lost them with that last little jump, Tom. Which means it can't zero in on our Mayday."

"Where is it now?"

"Starboard thirty-two will bring you in a straight-line angle. But it's moving off fast!"

"We'll fix that," Tom said. Glancing at the glowing digital direction display to his left, he pulled into a high, arcing loop that took him into a path over the night-side of earth. A storm front moved sluggishly over the South Atlantic. Night touched the western coast of Africa as the ship swept over darkened Europe and the pole, closing the gap between the *Exedra* and the orbit of *New America*.

"Those buzzards are right on our tail," Ben said tightly. "One about six o'clock, the other coming up on our belly!"

Tom slammed the *Exedra*'s throttle into the

red. The sleek craft shuddered as the big nuclear engines screamed with power. The awesome surge of energy hurled the ship over the far curve of Earth. Suddenly, the white-hot ball of the Sun flared against the blackness.

"We have to be close enough now," Tom shouted over the noise. "We're on the scopes in *New America*, you can bet on that! They'll—"

Twin lances of red stitched a deadly laser pattern in front of the ship. Tom reacted instantly, tossing the *Exedra* into a flat, dizzy spiral over the sky.

"Tom," Ben blurted suddenly, "the other two are still behind us. They've sucked us into a trap!"

Tom's heart sank. He knew Ben was right. There was a *third* enemy craft, climbing rapidly up on their tail.

Chapter Two

Tom's mind raced. "All right," he shouted. "I've had enough of this. Take over the controls, Ben. Keep 'er steady as long as you can!"

Passing the inert form of Aristotle, he jerked a spare rocket thruster from a port rack and snapped open the small panel in its side. From a locker, he took a metal box containing round, silver objects no larger than tennis balls. They were starflares, one of Tom's most recent inventions. Designed initially as survey spotters for the asteroid belt, he had a better use for them now.

Quickly, he jammed the starflares into the 17

rocket thruster, loaded it into a launch tube aft, and shoved himself back to Ben's side. He was barely strapped in before Ben yanked the *Exedra* into a series of twisting curves that set the craft spinning on its axis three hundred miles over the Pacific.

"Okay, pull out and shoot her up ninety degrees," Tom called out.

Ben thrust the *Exedra* straight up. "Oh, great," he moaned, "now we've got all *three* of 'em on our tail!"

"Good, said Tom, "that's right where I want 'em." He leaned over the panel and pulled a manual switch. The rocket thruster shot out the stern. "Lower your visor," Tom warned, *"quick!"*

The black-finned vessels closed fast. Lasers etched intersecting patterns against the darkness of space, searching out the *Exedra*. Then, three dozen starflares exploded at once, right in the path of the attackers.

The searing core of brightness expanded quickly, swelling to a globe of light nearly forty miles deep. The flash had no destructive power —the enemy's instruments would identify the enormous ball of light as a flare and nothing more. Still, their pursuers didn't need a scientific scan to tell them this miniature star would bring every patrol vessel in orbit to the scene. Circling the bright light once, they accelerated quickly and shot out of sight.

Less than half an hour later, the *Exedra* drifted into the docking port below the gleaming cylinder of *New America*, escorted by three shark-bowed craft of the Space Marines. A squat rescue tug grappled the ship and nudged it toward the starkly lit cavern of Bay Nine.

From a distance, *New America* looked small against the dark vastness of space. Closer, the awesome size of the orbiting colony became quite clear to the visitor. As often as Tom approached *New America*, he never failed to be overwhelmed by the immensity of the project. *New America* was three miles long and a mile in diameter. More than 50,000 people now lived and worked inside its metal shell. Lakes, farms, forests, industries, and dwellings followed the inner curve of the rotating cylinder.

But it was *Ark Two*, the recently finished addition to *New America*, that was of particular interest to the young inventor. Designed by him and his father, *Ark Two* consisted of nine ecological systems, each a miniature world in itself, containing rare animals, sea creatures, and plants from nearly every continent on Earth. The concept of preserving the planet's endangered species was a popular one, not only with Earth, but also with the other members of the Interplanet Council, who didn't always agree with Earth's other policies and projects.

Tom and Ben Walking Eagle stepped onto the latticed metal floor of Bay Nine. Admiral Ross Silmon glanced at the *Exedra*'s laser-scarred surface as he greeted them, concern spreading over his features.

"I'm not sure what happened out there," he said tightly, "but I'm glad to see you in one piece." He shook their hands and guided them quickly away from the craft.

"We're not too certain either, sir," said Tom. "But we're happy to be here."

Silmon said nothing more until the three reached his personal quarters. He was a tall, slim, black man with graying hair and a neatly clipped beard. Officially, he was head of the Space Marine contingent for both *New America* and *Sunflower*, a nearby torus-shaped colony now nearing completion. But Tom knew the admiral was also deeply involved in intelligence matters dealing with interplanet security.

"Let's get right to it," Silmon said, gesturing Tom and Ben to comfortable chairs. "We have a great deal to talk about. More, perhaps, than either of you imagine." He paused, letting his gaze move from one boy to the other. "You're not the only ones having 'accidents' and strange encounters these days. We've been experiencing some rather peculiar happenings here ourselves."

"What do you mean, sir?" Tom asked, curious.

Silmon held up a hand. "Can I hold off on that for a moment? Tell me exactly what went on out in space. All we know is that you were attacked by someone—or something. We got your Mayday and saw the light show you put on. Aside from that, I'm rather in the dark."

Tom told him all about the power overage that had put Aristotle and the shadowlator out of commission, and then the attack by the dark-finned vessels. When he was finished, Admiral Silmon got up from his chair and stared out of the big viewport at the distant blue marble of Earth.

"I've never heard of ships like that before," he said thoughtfully. "They aren't Interplanet craft, and they don't sound much like space pirates. Not the ones we've tangled with, in any case."

"We don't think so, either," Tom confided. "But whoever they were, they had plenty of horses in their power plants. I'd say they had more speed than a marine *Lancer* class fighter."

Admiral Silmon frowned, clasped his hands behind his back, and shook his head. "I don't like the sound of that. We got a quick readout on their speed, and didn't want to believe what we saw. Your data confirms it, I'm afraid."

"They're fast," Ben added. "And I can tell you, sir, their inboard computer gear is every bit as good as ours."

Silmon set his jaw and glanced sourly out the viewport. "You think they could have been after the shadowlator?" Silmon was one of the few people who knew the purpose of Tom's device.

"If they were," Tom said flatly, "they've got a funny way of going about it. If one of those lasers had hit the *Exedra*, there wouldn't be anything left to steal. Besides, other strange things happened lately." He described the lab fire in Triton dome, and the unexplained blowout at one of the dome's pressure doors.

Silmon's dark eyes bored into Tom. "You want to know what I think? I think it's the two of you these people are after. You and Ben Walking Eagle."

Tom and Ben sat up straight. "Why?" Ben asked. "What in the world for?"

"I don't know," Silmon said uneasily. "I think we'd better find out, though." He flicked the personal communicator on his wrist and spoke into it. "Joe, have our best techs go over the *Excedra* with a fine-tooth comb. I want to know exactly what put Tom Swift out of action."

"Are you thinking about sabotage, sir?" Tom asked when the admiral had finished.

A shadow crossed Silmon's face. "It's something we have to consider. Someone could've rigged your power system to overload so you'd be sitting ducks for those ships."

Ben was puzzled. "But who knew we were out there testing the shadowlator?" he asked. "Very few people even know the device exists."

"People at Swift Enterprises knew," Silmon pointed out.

"There are only eight or nine who had access to the data," Tom said. "If there's a spy, he must have pretty good connections. I just can't believe it."

Admiral Silmon shrugged. "I'm not saying it's so. But in the light of what's been happening up here . . ."

"You started to get into that, sir," Tom prompted.

Silmon stood up and ran a hand through his hair. "Some pretty peculiar things, Tom. In the first place—"

He was interrupted by a soft buzzing at his wrist. He spoke into the instrument, then looked at Tom, a slight smile touching the corners of his mouth. "There are a couple of people waiting outside. I think it'd be a good idea if they were in on this."

Before either Tom or Ben could comment, the door slid open. Standing in the portal were a beautiful red-haired girl and a blue-skinned alien from the waterworld of Aquilla.

"Anita! K'orlii!" Tom and Ben cried out and got up to greet their friends. Anita Thorwald had shared many space adventures with the two boys, and K'orlii was an old friend of theirs.

"Well!" Anita grinned, giving them both a friendly embrace. "Looks like you two can't stay out of trouble more than a couple of minutes at a time."

"You're right," Tom said. "We need your calm, steadying hand, Anita. Nothing ever happens when you're around."

Anita exploded into laughter. Tom's statement was anything but the truth. Action followed the fiery redhead wherever she went. Tom had first met her when his prototype fusion racer, the *Davy Cricket*, came up against Anita's *Valkyrie* in the Space Triangle competition. After a rather stormy beginning, they had become fast friends.

"I am grieved to hear you encountered trouble," K'orlii said. "You are both all right?"

"Fine, now," Tom assured him. "We weren't all that sure a few minutes ago."

The Aquillan was a sharp contrast to Anita Thorwald. Where the redhead was outgoing and quick to jump to a challenge, K'orlii was shy and reserved. As a native of a waterworld dotted with coral islands, he was as much at home in the sea as on land. The narrow, almost invisible slits at the base of his throat acted as gills underwater, while a healthy pair of Earthlike lungs served him on the surface. Except for the pale blue cast to his skin, he looked a great deal like a slim native of Earth. He had dark, shiny, black hair and the powerful shoulders of a swimmer. K'orlii's eyes were his most striking, and truly alien, feature. They were large, penetrating circles of gold, flecked with bright shards of aqua and silver.

K'orlii and Anita took seats, then Anita said, "Oh, Admiral, Captain Morgan stopped me in the hall with a message. Those ships that attacked the *Excedra* took off straight into Quadrant B. Deepspace radar followed them awhile and then lost them."

"Quadrant B?" Silmon bent his head in thought. "That's the general direction of the asteroid belt."

"Which makes them sound like pirates," Ben said.

"Or someone who wants us to *think* they're pirates," Silmon added. "I was just getting ready to tell you about what's been happening here on *New America*. Maybe you'd like to take over, Anita. You were one of the people who saw it."

Tom's chin came up. "Saw what? Where?"

"A strange guy was hanging around the access lock to *SeaGlobe*," she replied. "It was too dark to get a good look at him, and he wore a black cloak that covered his head. I noticed him twice. One of the maintenance technicians saw him again, just last night."

Tom frowned. "All three times around *Sea-Globe*? Never at any of the other ecosystems?"

"No." Anita shook her head. "And I couldn't get close enough to see what he was up to. Neither could the tech."

Tom let out a lungful of air. "Admiral, who'd want to bother the ecological stations? I can't imagine anyone harming the endangered species we—"

A loud alarm clanged through the halls outside, cutting off his words.

"Looks like someone disagrees with you!" shouted Anita.

Chapter Three

Ross Silmon bounded through the sliding door to the corridor, a short sonic weapon clutched in his fist. A marine snapped a quick salute and pointed down the hall. Tom and his friends followed the admiral a hundred yards along the narrow, yellow-striped corridor.

A guard was sitting up against the heavy steel lock to the *SeaGlobe* access area, blinking and shaking his head. An ugly bruise was forming over his right eye.

"What happened here, son?" Silmon bent over the man, concern clouding his features.

"Not . . . real sure." The man shook his head, and saw the rank on Silmon's shoulder. "—Sir," he added quickly.

27

"You get a glimpse who did it?"

"Sort of," the marine said hazily. "He had this cloak—"

"A black hood?"

"Yes, sir. But I—" The young guard hesitated, looked past Silmon, and pointed a shaky finger at K'orlii. "It was one of them, sir!" he said angrily. "I got enough of a look to know that!"

"No." K'orlii shook his head firmly. "I—know it wasn't an Aquillan!"

"I saw him," the marine insisted. "Plain as day, sir. Heard him come up behind me, and when I turned, there was this blue face looking right at me. And those big, yellow eyes!"

A group of marines had gathered about. Two of them helped the guard to his feet and guided him toward the nearest infirmary. Admiral Silmon ordered the others to start a search.

"I don't know if it'll turn up anything, but we'll give it a try," he said.

"Admiral," K'orlii said intently, "I do not think an Aquillan could be involved in this. It is not impossible, but it does not seem logical, does it?"

Silmon's eyes narrowed. "Logical? Why do you say that?"

"Simply because it would not make sense for one of my people to break into *SeaGlobe*." K'orlii spread his hands. "Every Aquillan on *New Ameri-*

ca already *has* access to that area. That is our major responsibility here. Tending the sea creatures of Earth."

"Hmmm." Silmon bit his lip. "You're right." He paused a long moment. "I want to be fair about this," he said finally. "But I have to consider the evidence. You understand that."

"Yes, sir. Quite clearly," K'orlii said.

"I know the corporal who got hit. He's a good marine. A reliable man. He wouldn't make up a story like that." Silmon sighed and looked down the corridor. Tom could tell from his expression that he didn't want to believe Aquillans were involved any more than K'orlii did. "Let's see what turns up, all right?" With a nod to Tom and his friends, he stalked quickly back down the tunnel, rounded a corner, and disappeared.

"Look." Anita Thorwald flashed them all a cheery grin. "We have some time before third dinner. I've got something to show you down in *KenyaWorld*. Come with me and then we'll eat. Okay?"

K'orlii looked less than enthusiastic, but Tom and Ben pulled him along. The Aquillan didn't care to see a small piece of the African veldt right now, Tom knew, but he didn't need to be alone, either.

Tom had been to *KenyaWorld* before, but never

tired of the place. Like all the ecosystems, it was loosely tethered to *New America* at the end of a delicate metal lattice. Each globe rotated on its own within a socketlike frame. A five-foot-wide, mesh-free band circled it to allow access inside. A suctioned airlock slid constantly over the surface, offering a ten-second entry time before it sealed itself.

Tom blinked in the sudden brightness of the African "sun," filtered through transparent strips on the globe for the appropriate density of light and heat. The hot, yellow grassland under his feet stretched up to the curve of the dome, gave way to a thick grove of trees and then a bright blue lake directly overhead.

"Look, over there!" Anita Thorwald grabbed Tom's arm and pointed excitedly across the plain. A small herd of gazelles bounded through the grass, leaping high in the air as if their hooves were spring-loaded. The airy little animals disturbed a pair of grazing eland. The big, ugly beasts snorted and rumbled off.

Even K'orlii seemed to toss his troubles aside. He stared in wonder at the spectacular vista before him. "If this is any example," he told Anita, "I would like to see the real Africa sometime!"

"No, you wouldn't." Anita frowned. "It's not much like this anymore. Unfortunately. That's what *KenyaWorld*'s for, of course. And the other domes as well. We're preserving what we can up here, while the job of cleaning up Earth goes on below."

K'orlii pointed to two giant African elephants lumbering out of the forest nearby. One flipped its ears in a challenge and the other one raised its trunk and trumpeted loudly.

"Shouldn't we—ah—move out of their way?" K'orlii suggested.

"Not necessary," Anita said. "Sonic barriers keep the species apart. From each other, and from us. We can't afford to have predators swallowing up a whole endangered species in one tasty meal."

She grinned and winked at K'orlii's horrified expression. "Don't worry, the really tough customers here, like the big cats, all wear safecollars. One of Tom's inventions. Kind of a personal micro-sonic element that keeps the beasts relatively calm."

"How calm is—relatively calm?" Ben asked.

"You mean, will the lions eat North American Indians?"

"Yes. Something like that."

Anita shrugged and motioned him to follow. "Why don't we wander over to Section D? It's easy enough to find out."

Ben looked at her suspiciously and stood his

ground. He knew Anita Thorwald well, but wasn't sure how far she'd go to prove her point.

"Sounds like a good idea to me," said Tom.

Ben shot him a look. "Who asked you?"

K'orlii and Tom laughed.

"No, seriously," said Anita, leading them toward the trees, "we do have a lot of big cats here, and the place isn't so large that we don't watch them carefully. There's a mix here, you know. Not everything in *KenyaWorld* is from Africa. For lack of space, we have to bunch the general climatic zones together."

Four leathery crocodiles slid into the water at their approach, and Tom saw a distant pair of hippos disappear under the muddy surface.

Anita found a spare electric rover, and they all piled aboard.

In half an hour, they had gone up the side of the globe to the edge of a wide lake bordered by reeds and high grasses. Another rover passed them, and Anita waved to the two girls in it. Both wore chrome-yellow jumpsuits like Anita's— standard dress for *KenyaWorld* staff.

"Okay," she said finally, bringing the rover to a halt. "Everybody out, only take it easy and don't move too fast. The animals I want you to see are rather shy."

She started around the corner of the lake,

guiding the others through shoulder-high reeds that rustled like paper as the young people passed. For a while, neither Tom nor his friends could see a thing. Then, the reeds began to thin, and Anita put a finger to her lips. "No talking from here on in," she whispered. She walked another few yards; then, as she parted the reeds gently, a satisfied smile touched her lips. "Take a look. All of you. You'll never see another sight like this."

Tom moved up, peering over Ben's shoulder. Across the narrow arm of a lake, broad, flat grasslands stretched far up the curve of the globe. In the center of the plain stood two tall, perfectly straight trees with high, bushy crowns. As Tom watched, one of them moved. Then the other.

Tom beamed. "You're right, Anita. It's something to see!"

K'orlii was puzzled. "Wh—what are they?"

Anita laughed gently. "They're giraffes, K'orlii. A male and a female. The only ones in existence. That's one of the things that makes them very special. The other is that we *hope* maybe there'll be a baby giraffe soon!"

The two animals loped easily across the plain at right angles to the watchers. Knobby legs ate up the yards, while the long, graceful necks bobbed along above.

"The male's eighteen feet high," Anita said.

"He—Oh, *no*!" Suddenly, she went rigid. Tom saw the shock and fear in her eyes and squinted in the direction of the giraffes. The big, gangly creatures turned in mid-stride, wheeled about, and raced frantically toward the lake.

Another animal streaked across the veldt behind the giraffes. It was a large bundle of yellow and black muscle, bounding like the wind and cutting the grass like waves.

"It's a Bengal!" Tom shouted. "A big one! Anita, what's it *doing* out there?"

"I—don't know. If it gets those giraffes—" Her face clouded with anger. Before Tom could stop her, she stepped out of the reeds, shouting and waving her arms. "You *quit* that, you hear! Get away from those animals right this minute!"

"Anita!" Ben stared in horror, reached out, and pulled her back to cover. Anita blinked. It suddenly dawned on her what she was doing. Seventy yards away, the enormous tiger stopped, turned toward the reeds, and sniffed the air.

"*Uh*-oh." Anita bit her lips and let out a groan. "Real sorry about that, folks. Time to leave now. Just follow me and *don't* fall behind!"

Ben jerked a thumb over his shoulder. "Just where is it we're going that—*he* can't?"

Anita didn't answer. She walked quickly through the reeds, talking rapidly into the personal com-unit on her wrist. Tom knew she was scared, and trying hard not to show it.

"Where is he?" she said evenly, without looking back. "Can anyone see him?"

"He's still with us," said Tom. "Had him a minute ago but I lost him."

"Don't *run*," she told them. "Just keep walking and don't stop. I've called a hover-patrol. We'll get help."

"Where are they?" K'orlii asked anxiously. "Close by, I hope?"

Anita sighed. "No, to be honest, they're not close at all. But they'll be here. . . . Look—I'm sorry about this. It was a stupid thing to do."

"You were worried about the giraffes," said Tom. "Nobody blames you for that."

"*I* do!" Anita said hotly. "Giraffes are one thing. People are something else!" Her fists tightened into knots and a fiery red curl fell in her face. "Dumb," she fumed, "dumb, dumb, dumb!"

"You've got my vote," Ben said beside her.

Anita shot him a look. "For once, Ben Stumbling Eagle, you're right. But don't press your luck, okay?"

Suddenly, the high river weeds gave way to open ground again. Anita kept walking, holding a fast, steady pace. The edge of the forest seemed impossibly far away—a good 200 yards over ground with no cover.

"We can get a tranquilizer gun from the rover," she said. "Only thing is, I don't think that cat's going to wait that long."

"Maybe he stopped in the reeds," Ben said hopefully. "Or turned around and took off for the giraffes—"

A deep, throaty roar echoed from the river.

"Oh, no!" Ben groaned.

The tiger bellowed once more, much closer this time. Then, suddenly, the reeds behind them gave way. The Bengal leaped out into the open, set its enormous paws, and bounded straight for them, its great striped head bunched low under its shoulders.

"Now you can run!" Anita screamed.

"Spread out," Tom snapped, "don't bunch up!"

Tom, Anita, Ben, and K'orlii ran off, weaving zigzag patterns toward the rover. For a split-second, the Bengal paused, confused at the four dinners moving away in separate paths. Then, it turned its gleaming eyes on Tom Swift, corded its big flanks, and charged through the grass.

Tom heard Anita yell, and looked quickly behind him. Something turned to lead in his stomach. The tiger was close—*too* close! It ate up the yards between them. Forty . . . twenty . . .

The Bengal strained on its haunches and leaped. Tom hit the ground and buried his face. He felt the carnivore's breath, and saw it hit the ground not three feet away. Massive jaws opened in a roar. Suddenly, the tiger's eyes went blank. The animal teetered, then slumped to the ground.

Tom rose shakily to his feet. He heard the soft whir of a hover overhead and glanced up. A man in a yellow jumpsuit peered anxiously over the side, a stubby tranquilizer gun still clutched in his hands. Then the craft veered off and came to the ground a few yards away.

Tom and the others walked up to the tiger. It was even bigger up close.

"Look at that," Anita said intently. She pointed at the sleeping animal. "It—doesn't have a safe-collar. That's impossible—they *can't* get those things off!"

Tom wiped a hand over his face. "Anita, did you tell *any*one we were coming here?"

"Why, yes. Of course. Lots of people. I've been planning to show you the giraffes, and—" she stopped, letting her words trail away. "Oh, *no*!"

"I'm not sure why," Tom said evenly, "but someone wants us all dead. One way or another . . ."

Chapter Four

After the incident at *KenyaWorld*, Tom and his friends decided to stay out of *Ark Two*'s crowded staff dining room. Instead, they picked up sandwiches and went into the small lab Tom used during his stays in *New America*.

Anita Thorwald received a call on her personal com-unit and reported to the others. She said, "It wasn't just the safecollar. Someone messed with the sonic barrier system as well." She searched for a pencil and paper, then cleared a space on Tom's workbench. "Look—the system's laid out like this: the animals' territories flow in and out of each other—like different colors of paint that don't mix. You know? It's pretty much the way it occurs in nature, except there's a *lot* of mingling there. On *KenyaWorld*, this means everybody who needs to can get to grasslands, water, trees—whatever's called for in their natural environments."

Anita laid down the pencil. "Whoever sicced that Bengal on us knew exactly what he was doing. According to the computer boys, he practically *herded* that tiger into our laps! Just pushed him along right into the giraffes' territory."

Tom scowled over his sandwich. "That calls for some pretty sophisticated knowledge. In more than one field, too."

"Does that surprise anyone?" Ben asked. "Whoever's behind all this—and I'm assuming it's the same gang—knows about the shadowlator, the way pressure doors work at the dome, has a knowledge of sonics—and access to a bunch of high-powered spaceships equipped with laser weapons."

"Not exactly a nickel-and-dime outfit," Tom agreed. "The thing that keeps eating at me is—*why*? Whoever these people are, what do they want?"

"Oh, I almost forgot," Anita put in. She looked at K'orlii. "I found out that no Aquillan has been in *KenyaWorld* for the last six *weeks*. So they can't say any of your people were responsible for this."

"Which doesn't mean a lot, I'm afraid." K'orlii

shrugged. "If this gang is as widespread as it appears to be, there *could* be some Aquillans involved. I just don't believe it, that's all!"

Next day, Ben and K'orlii had chores to do, while Anita and Tom went to the lab to work on Aristotle. The attractive redhead was knowledgeable in a number of fields, but her area of expertise was null-gravity prosthetics. As a result of an accident, Anita had an artificial leg from the knee down that included a complete computer terminal and in no way handicapped her athletic capabilities. Her personal experience with a bionic limb made her invaluable for a task like the present one.

"Well, I don't think I can add much to your diagnosis, Doctor Swift." Anita sighed and switched off the magnified view of a portion of the robot's damaged circuits. "Friend Aristotle does *not* look well. That power surge on the *Exedra* barbecued the old boy, but good." She picked up a fused component and glared at it distastefully. "Do you have spares for all this, by any chance? We might as well get to it."

Tom caught her expression and laid a hand on her shoulder. "It won't be as bad as it looks." He grinned. "Not with your magic leg around to help."

Anita looked puzzled, then her face suddenly brightened. "Of course! Why didn't I think of that? We can run all the information through my test circuits and keep an up-to-date picture of how we're doing."

"Cleaning up the basic unit's the hardest part," Tom added. "If you can get us through that, we'll let Aristotle himself take over some of the work. If he's testing his own components, that'll cut the job in half."

"Maybe." Anita pushed back her hair and gave him a dubious look. "You know Thorwald's Law, don't you? Everything takes twice as long as it should."

"Except for the parts that appear easy," Tom added. "Those take *three* times as long."

Anita was right. Even with shortcuts, the job of restoring the robot took a good part of the day. Once Aristotle was fully functioning, Tom filled him in on the events that had taken place since his burnout. Aristotle's memory circuits were totally intact up to that point. Part of the robot's value lay in his continual accumulation of data, and the more he knew, the more helpful he could be. In designing Aristotle, Tom had made certain the memory circuits were properly shielded against anything short of the robot's total destruction.

Tom stood back and looked him over. "Well, how do you feel, old friend?"

Aristotle's cobalt and lavender sensors flickered once. "As I understand, Tom, your question refers to my physical well-being. I am intact and in good working order, thank you. Anita, I greet you once again."

"And I—ah—greet you too, Aristotle."

"Obviously, unknown forces are determined to hamper or destroy you and your friends, Tom. Unless you have failed to give me all available data, I find these continued attacks totally illogical. Human aggression is usually motivated by some real or imagined need."

"That's our conclusion, too," Tom said. "But, as I've mentioned before, logic doesn't have all that much to do with the way humans act."

"Most unfortunate," Aristotle commented.

Tom instructed the robot to triple-check his components and circuits, then joined Anita across the lab.

She glanced past him and raised a curious brow. "Is that rig what I think it is? Looks familiar."

"This?" Tom turned to the workbench behind him, and picked up a narrow, mesh-metal belt. Nylon webbed straps were attached to it, and held a flat, lightweight box curved to fit the human back. He handed it to Anita. "I've got several of these made up. If things quiet down around here we can give them a try tomorrow."

"It *is* the drysuit, isn't it?" Anita beamed. "You got it finished, Tom! Does it work?"

"It works fine, but I'd like you and Ben to test it, too. There are always a couple of minor bugs to work out. We'll go out to *SeaGlobe* in the morning."

"I'd really love to. Tom, this is going to make scuba diving something that nearly anyone could do!"

"I hope it'll do more than that," Tom said. "If I can get the pressure problems worked out, we'll have a good safety suit for deepspace work, as well as underwater exploring."

The drysuit was an invention Tom had been working on during his stay at Triton dome. Intricate microcircuits in the belt itself created an oxygenated field around the wearer—a "dry" envelope of air that enabled him to breathe and move about freely without cumbersome masks and equipment. Lightweight, high-pressure oxygen tanks were the only additional gear necessary.

Anita turned the belt over in her hands, studying it carefully. "I know it works if you say it does," she said. "Guess it'll take a little time though, to get up the nerve to just dive in without a mask and start breathing."

"You'll get used to it," Tom assured her. "As you say, it takes a little time. Before long, we'll all be swimming like K'orlii."

"Hah!" Anita raised a brow at that. "I've *seen* Aquillans swim, Tom, and I'm not ready to compete! Drysuit or not."

The com on Tom's wrist buzzed. He listened to it, answered, and turned to Anita. "That was Admiral Silmon," he said slowly. "He wants us over at his place. Now. Ben and K'orlii will meet us there."

"Is something wrong?"

"Could be, from the way he sounded."

Tom locked the lab with his own fingerprint code, leaving Aristotle inside. He and Anita quickly walked to the nearest aircycle station. A technician in a red jumpsuit passed them, glanced at them briefly, then hurried on in the opposite direction.

The two friends each got an aircycle, which was the major mode of transportation on *New America*, and rode to Admiral Silmon's office. They left their cycles at a station around the corner. When they got off, Tom suddenly took Anita's arm.

"See that guy in red?" he whispered, pointing to a man disappearing around the next bend.

"What about him?"

"He passed us in front of the lab and, even though he was going in the opposite direction, he got here before us!"

Anita stared at her friend. "You mean he's shadowing us?"

"Not only that. The only way he could have beaten us here is through the security emergency tube. Which means he's got pretty high clearance."

"Let's see where he went!" Anita said, and both broke into a run. When they rounded the corner, they saw the man duck into a doorway.

Tom and Anita followed. They found themselves in a small shop specializing in cheeses and breads. The man was not there!

"May I help you?" The pretty brunette behind the counter smiled. "I was about to close up, but—"

"The man who came in here. Where'd he go?"

Just then, the door behind Tom jerked open. The man in the red jumpsuit stopped and blinked in surprise. Tom saw a quick flash of anger in his eyes.

"Anita!" He yelled out a warning as the man's hand reached into his pocket. Tom came in low with his shoulders in a football crouch. The gleaming needle gun went off in the man's hand. Tom felt the small-finned missiles whistle by his

46

head as his shoulder slammed into the gunman's midsection. Then he crashed to the floor.

The man lost his footing and was thrown against the door frame. The weapon fell out of his hand and onto the plastic walkway. But he regained his balance and ran outside. Tom scrambled to his feet and rushed after him. The gunman apparently knew the neighborhood well. He took two quick turns down twisting byways and vanished in a crowd of shoppers. Tom gave up, disgusted, and went back to the shop.

Meanwhile, Anita was trying desperately to explain things to the clerk. It wasn't an easy task, as the man had emptied his whole clip inside the shop. Round cheeses, loaves of fresh-baked bread, and hanging sausages were studded with sharp projectiles.

When Tom walked in, she turned anxiously toward him. "Are you all right?"

"I'm fine, but that creep got away," Tom said. "Sorry about all the excitement," he told the clerk. "If there's any damage, we'll be glad to take care of it."

"No—that's all right." The girl forced a nervous smile. "You folks—come back any time —if you're looking for cheese, that is. . . ."

"That just about does it," Tom said angrily

when they reached Silmon's office. "Whoever these people are, Admiral, they've started a small war right here in *New America*!"

He paced the room, his hands jammed in his pockets. Ben leaned against the far wall, while Anita and K'orlii sat across from Admiral Silmon.

"I wish I could tell you what's going on around here," Silmon said. "Unfortunately, all I can do is add to the confusion."

Tom looked up uneasily, noticing the worry lines around the admiral's eyes. "I have an idea none of us are going to like this. Now what?"

Admiral Silmon opened a shallow drawer in his desk and dropped a small silver ring on the flat, white surface. K'orlii gasped, picked it up, and stared at it.

"Sir, where did you get this?"

"You can tell me what it is, I guess," said Silmon.

"Yes, sir. Of course I can. It's a ring, with the house sign of my family on it. I have one just like it." He held up his hand and showed them the crested silver ring. "Where did this come from, Admiral?"

"That's the bad part of it. My search team found it in the corridor. Not thirty yards from where that guard was knocked out this morning."

"I don't believe that!" K'orlii blurted. His golden eyes flashed. "There are no other members of my family clan on *New America*!"

"I know that," the admiral said softly. "Nevertheless, the ring *is* here, isn't it?"

"It doesn't prove anything, K'orlii," Tom said. He turned quickly to Silmon. "It's more than a little peculiar, don't you think so, sir? First, the guard sees an Aquillan face. Then, later, we conveniently find an Aquillan ring. Rings don't just drop off people's fingers. That's not too subtle, is it?"

"No, it's not." Admiral Silmon stood up and sighed. "Now, you want to hear the rest of it?"

"There's more?"

"Afraid so. And none of it good. One, I just got a call from Swift Enterprises. A technical employee is missing from Triton dome. He worked at your father's headquarters in Shopton on the mainland, then transfered to Triton dome less than four weeks ago." Silmon looked at Tom. "Just before the *accidents* in the dome, and in your lab."

"Another coincidence," Tom said drily.

"Exactly. And two—" This time Silmon looked at K'orlii. "I hate to keep piling bad news on you, but here it is. The pictures our deepspace probes got of those three ships that attacked the *Exedra*

49

weren't very clear, but they were good enough for a positive I.D. Those fins fooled us for a while. Take 'em off and the silhouette's convincing enough. The ships were Aquillan, without a doubt."

Chapter Five

Later that day, Tom and his friends floated above the access lock to *SeaGlobe*. Tom curled up into a ball and kicked his legs to stop his motion. He grabbed a handhold and glanced over his shoulder. Ben, Anita, and K'orlii were just behind him, clearing the last fifty yards of the narrow tunnel.

Tom turned back to the lock and stared at the great, milky-blue moon of *SeaGlobe*. The waterworld ecosystem was a vast, luminous pearl against the velvet of space. It swallowed all of the heavens, blanking out the stars. Among the components of *Ark Two*, only *KenyaWorld* was larger.

The others came up behind him and Ben gave

a long, appreciative whistle. "Now *that* is what I'd call one big aquarium."

"I'd hate to have to change the water," Anita quipped. She brushed her hair aside. "Ready for a swim, friend?"

"We will be," Tom said, "after I get everybody checked out on the equipment."

There had been no need for the standard rubber suits, even though they would dive to considerable depths. The boys wore swim trunks, and Anita had on a blue bikini. The envelope of air created by the drysuit not only held back the water, but also enabled the body to maintain a comfortable temperature at different depths and pressures.

Crouched before the access lock, Tom moved around his friends for a final check. Small READY lights on each of the mesh-metal belts winked blue. Nylon webbing held the compact instrument packs snugly between the divers' shoulders. Tom had rigged cylinders of oxy-mix to the sides of the packs. The mix was highly compressed, and each cylinder was no larger than an old-fashioned thermos.

"When we activate inside," Tom said, "the second light on your belt will show yellow. That means you're breathing in the oxygenated pressure field."

"*If* this thing works," said Ben.

Tom grinned. "If it doesn't, K'orlii will pull you out and you get your money back."

He pushed himself off and floated the last few feet through the entry. Outside, shiny strips of light flashed by, part of the spidery metal lattice that held *SeaGlobe* in its tethered orbit.

Finally, the long tunnel ended at the suctioned access portal that slid continually across the globe's surface. The elliptical pressure door opened, and the young people pulled themselves inside. There was a slow transition from weightlessness to the approximate surface gravity of Earth, and the cool, machine-circulated air of the tunnel gave way to the warmer, heavy atmosphere of *SeaGlobe*. They climbed down the short ladder to a hollow metal platform floating on the water. *SeaGlobe*'s aqua-green surface curved away and disappeared under a translucent plastic sky.

"Takes some getting used to," Anita said. "You get accustomed to walking up the *in*side of a sphere in the other ecosystems."

K'orlii dove past the pair and disappeared under a trail of frothy bubbles. The water was clear and Tom could see him just below—a pale blue streak against a dark green.

He activated his drysuit, lowered himself over the platform, and stuck his head tentatively under the water. The suit worked perfectly. It was an eerie feeling, gazing at the underwater world without a scuba outfit or mask. He felt as if an invisible sheet of glass followed the curve of his body an inch above his skin.

Ben joined him, then Anita. She grinned broadly, kicking her arms and legs to stay in place. "It's fantastic, I have to admit it." Her voice reached him loud and clear through his earstud receivers.

"Look—over there," said Ben.

A hundred yards to the left, three blue-skinned Aquillans rode herd on a school of tuna. As Tom watched, the whole school turned abruptly in a single flash of silver, then scattered out of sight into the depths.

"A pair of great whites just to port," K'orlii said casually. "I imagine that's what spooked the tuna."

Ben eyed the distant sharks warily. "I can understand that."

"*SeaGlobe*'s predators are outfitted with an underwater version of the safecollar," Anita put in. "They won't bother us."

"That Bengal was supposed to have a safecollar, too," Ben noted.

Anita shook her head. "Not the same thing, friend. Someone took the collar off him. He didn't do it himself."

Tom moved away, plunging deep below the shallows. He knew what Ben was afraid of. There had been several attempts on their lives already. Why not another in *SeaGlobe*? It was an ideal spot for an "accident." And if the Aquillans were really involved—

Tom didn't like to think about that. Most of the Aquillans he'd met were a great deal like K'orlii —polite, reserved, and definitely peace-loving.

Who, then? Tom wondered. All the star races were basically friendly to man. Space pirates were a continual headache, but they lacked both the size and the organization for a job like this. If David Luna were still around, Tom thought, I'd lay the blame at his door. Their archenemy, a billionaire industrialist who had made his money by less than honest means, would have been capable of anything and wouldn't stop short of even murder to get what he wanted. Luna, though, was most likely dead. After their adventure in *The Rescue Mission,* his ship had last been seen in a space fight with the Sansoth, an alien life form, and there had been nothing anyone could do to save him.

By some miracle, had he escaped and returned to the Inner Planets to harrass Swift Enterprises?

A school of red and yellow fish parted in the trio's path. Below, Tom glimpsed the steadily darkening water. *SeaGlobe* was artificially pressurized to match Earth's ocean conditions. At the core of the system was a black, inky depth simulating a 10,000-foot Pacific trench. Large squid and enormous deep-sea eels lurked there, as well as delicate, violet-tinged sea lilies and some of Earth's only surviving giant clams.

"Tom—" Ben's voice crackled in his ear. "Come down here—you've got to see this!"

Tom glanced below and noticed a flash of Ben's coppery skin.

He and Anita were waiting under a cluster of vivid red millepore coral, a living forest that stretched down into the blue. Ben's eyes were wide with wonder at the sight.

"I didn't expect all this!" he said excitedly. "I thought *SeaGlobe* was just an overgrown fish tank."

"It's a lot more than that," Tom said. "It has to be, to simulate normal ocean conditions."

Tom had been amazed at *SeaGlobe*'s reef system himself, the first time he'd seen it. Coral reefs were vital to the survival of thousands of sea creatures—yet, *SeaGlobe* had no ocean "floor" to serve as a base for these growths. The problem had been solved in an ingenious manner. Instead of growing from the bottom, *SeaGlobe*'s coral literally ringed the entire system at the proper depths.

Tom followed Ben and Anita through the countless arches and tunnels of the living network. The reef blazed with color—white, pink, lavender, and flaming red. Delicately laced sea fans rippled in the lazy ocean current.

Anita came up beside him. "See that thing that looks like a cloud over there? It's a gigantic school of fairy shrimp."

Tom saw movement out of the corner of his eye. "It *used* to be, you mean."

A small school of yellow jack darted like missiles out of the deep and exploded into the shrimp. The pink cloud vanished, scattering in every direction. The jack circled about hungrily, quickly picking off the survivors.

"No safecollars on those babies," Ben said. "I know everybody eats somebody else in the ocean —but how does the personnel here make sure some valuable species doesn't get swallowed up overnight? Anita, you mentioned that problem in *KenyaWorld*."

Tom, Ben, and Anita turned to see K'orlii floating just above them. "I can answer that," K'orlii put in. "That's part of the job of the Aquillans working here. Our computers maintain a continual check on the food-chain balance. If anything gets too far out of line, field personnel set up sonic 'pens' to allow the diminished species to replenish itself." K'orlii paused and cocked his head as if some sound had suddenly alerted his senses. "Would you like to follow me? A couple of our biggest food-chain consumers are very close by!"

The trio tried hard to keep up with the Aquillan's natural speed through the water. They were all first-class swimmers, but none came close to matching K'orlii's pace. Finally, the Aquillan stopped and pointed straight up. "There—take a look at the lords of *SeaGlobe*."

"Good grief!" Anita backed off in awe and craned her neck upward. Two dark shapes the size of small submarines blotted out the light overhead.

"Sperm whales, right?" Tom said. "That one on the left must be sixty feet long."

"Seventy-two, to be exact," K'orlii corrected. "We have a herd of razorback whales as well. Some of them go up to a hundred feet or more."

"And I thought I had problems with elephants," Anita said drily. "What are those men doing with them, K'orlii? Looks like something's wrong with that big one's side."

"You're right. There is. She had a run-in with an overeager shark. Not a very common occurrence, really. Creatures this size don't have any natural enemies."

The whales hung lazily in the water, their enormous flippers barely moving in the current.

The four Aquillans worked on the big cow, administering antibiotics to the yard-long scar on her side. She didn't seem to care, but Tom noted she kept one tiny eye on the small beings hovering about her.

"Do they have safecollar implants, or what?" asked Anita. "She's taking all this rather calmly."

"No," K'orlii told her. "It's not necessary. We work so closely with the whale population, they're used to having us around."

"Kind of like my hippos, I guess. You can almost—"

Anita never finished. Suddenly, a violent tremor shook the water. Tom knew that an earthquake was impossible. The great whales reacted instantly. Their flippers lashed through the water and they dove for the depths, flinging their keepers aside.

"Quick—!" K'orlii's voice crackled in Tom's ears. "Back to the shallows!"

Tom saw fear cross the Aquillan's features. Then K'orlii was gone, leading them to the surface. Another tremor jolted the deep, this one far greater than the first. A shock wave of water hit Tom, slamming him head over heels. Anita yelled and tumbled past him. He reached out and grabbed her hand. Anita righted herself and followed.

The water brightened above. A school of frightened barracuda streaked by like bullets. A cloud of small yellow fish scattered and sped away.

Tom's head broke above water. The float was only twenty yards away. K'orlii was already there, frantically motioning to the others. He helped Ben up beside him, then Tom scrambled over the side and pulled Anita out of the water.

"Look out!" Ben shouted. "Here comes another one!" Tom and his companions threw themselves to the surface of the float. A tremendous shudder hit *SeaGlobe*. The float lifted up and slammed back into the waves, nearly spilling them all back into the water.

"Wh-what's *happening*?" gasped Anita. "Did we hit something? That's impossible!"

Before Tom could answer, an ominous tremor shook the translucent shell up above. Tom stared at the curving surface. Just beyond were two dark blurs, enormous shadows of something hovering over *SeaGlobe*.

"Out of the lock—quick!" he shouted, and scampered up the short ladder as fast as he could. The elliptical doors sighed open and he herded the others through, snapped the entry tight behind him, and raced for the access lock to the tunnel. The mechanism seemed to take forever to open. Finally, the four were through and into null-gravity flight down the long corridor to *New America*.

For the first time, Tom risked a look over his shoulder, and his heart dropped into the pit of his stomach. Two giant vessels hovered over *SeaGlobe*, one so close he could almost reach out and touch it. They were black, warty ships, their surfaces clustered with stubby spikes and fins. Flexible metal snouts hung from their bows and snaked over the surface of *SeaGlobe*. As Tom watched, round, flat discs grew at the end of these snouts and clamped themselves firmly to *SeaGlobe*'s milky shell.

Hair raised on the back of Tom's neck. Grasping a handhold, he threw himself down the passage. *"Hurry,"* he snapped at the others over his com, *"get out of here fast!"*

But he knew they'd never make it. The tunnel was a good mile and a half long. Before they reached the safety of *New America*, the dark vessels would slice the spidery network between *SeaGlobe* and the colony. When that happened, air would rush out of the tunnel and suck them into the vacuum of space. Tom knew what those snouts and grapple-discs were for. The intruders were there to steal *SeaGlobe* by shearing it away from *New America*'s grasp!

Chapter Six

Even without gravity to hold him back, Tom felt as if he were crawling through molasses. *New America* was still a thousand yards away now, a distance that might as well have been a thousand miles.

Suddenly, the flexible tunnel trembled, whipped like a snake, and slammed Tom hard against the wall. The momentum bounced him off one side and then another. He grabbed a handhold before the tumbling knocked him senseless. Darkness blocked out the stars. Tom shrank back: one of the black vessels hovered right over his head above the tether! A port winked open in a squat, ugly turret. For an instant, Tom saw a face bathed in harsh, blue light. The turret moved, swiveled in his direction. His throat went dry. He forced his hands off the girder and hurtled down the passage.

The lock was close, but not close enough. Ben, who was ahead of him with the others, stopped. He shoved Anita and K'orlii on before him and turned back to Tom.

"Ben, *don't*," Tom called out. "Get back—there's nothing you can do!"

"Can't hear you too well," Ben's voice sounded in his earstud. "Keep coming, Tom—don't stop now!" Ben plunged toward him, waving his arms. Red light winked from the ship. A razor-thin beam knifed through the darkness.

"Lasers!" Tom shouted. "They're slicing the tunnel!" He jerked to a halt and tangled his arms and legs around a network of metal. A small tornado howled through the passage, sucking every breath of air into space. The jolt nearly tore Tom from his perch. Instinctively, he jabbed a small button on the belt of his drysuit, swelling the envelope of air around his body. He knew it wouldn't work for long. The suit was built for underwater pressures, not for the awful vacuum of space.

Ben tumbled down the corridor heading straight for him. Tom reached out his hand and his friend slammed into him hard, nearly tearing Tom's arm out of its socket. Tom caught a quick glimpse of Ben's pale face. Frantically, he searched for the button on Ben's belt and pushed it. Ben took a deep swallow of air. Color came back to his cheeks.

"Some—rescue job, huh?"

"Terrific. You okay?"

"No, I'm *not* okay. I'm freezing to death. Tom, how are we—"

"The drysuits are holding back the pressure. They won't last more than another minute, though. The circuits will burn out and we'll explode all over *New America*!"

Ben jabbed a finger over Tom's shoulder. "Look!"

Tom turned. *SeaGlobe* shimmered, pulsing with a strange green light. Then it melted into the darkness of space!

Before Tom could comment, Ben shoved him down the tunnel and pushed after him. A numbing cold seeped through their bones. Tom knew the suits were failing, draining the small power packs on their backs. The lock was twenty yards away—too far!

Suddenly, yellow light filled the passage. Spacesuited figures darted toward them, their booster units streaming icy vapor. The rescuers jerked to a halt, grabbed Tom and Ben, and shot back to the lock. The heavy door slammed shut behind them, and pressurized air flooded the small room on the other side.

Sliding to the floor, Tom leaned wearily against a bulkhead and clicked off his drysuit. Ben grinned weakly and did the same. The marines took off their helmets and one turned to Tom.

"That was a little closer than I like 'em," he said. "But apparently that gadget of yours works."

Tom recognized the craggy features of Captain Marc Henson. "Up to about three minutes in a vacuum," he said shakily. "I wouldn't recommend more than that. Thanks for the quick job, Captain."

Henson shrugged, then snapped a quick salute as the inner lock opened and Admiral Silmon burst into the chamber, Anita and K'orlii at his heels. He looked the two over and let out a sigh of relief.

"I see you're alive," he said bluntly. "Not certain just how you did it, though."

Anita and K'orlii handed Tom and Ben blankets. Silmon asked no questions until a security carrier had whisked them back to his quarters, where they were served cups of hot tea.

"They got away clear," Silmon fumed. "Lured our patrols all over the quadrant with a false echo." He made no attempt to hide his anger. "Can anyone tell me *why* someone would want *SeaGlobe*? What can they do with it? They can't sell the thing!"

"Ransom, maybe," Anita suggested.

Silmon snorted. "Sure. That's possible. The project took a long time, and several billion dollars, to build. On top of that, the creatures in that globe are irreplaceable." He sighed and sank down in his chair.

"I don't know," Tom said hesitantly. "If this business has anything to do with what else has been happening, it doesn't make much sense. The incidents at Triton dome, the sabotaging of the shadowlator and the *Exedra*—" Tom spread his hands. "If stealing *SeaGlobe* was the objective, why bother with all the other stuff?"

"You're right," Ben agreed. "It doesn't fit." He took a swallow of tea. "I think it's something bigger. Something we're not seeing as yet."

"But what?" Anita asked. She stood up in agitation and paced around the room. "Tom, those vessels—"

"You saw it too, huh?"

"Well, I was rather far away," Anita said reluctantly.

Tom faced K'orlii. "I'm sorry, friend. There was an Aquillan aboard one of those ships."

K'orlii jumped to his feet. "Or someone who looked like one of us, Tom!" He ran a hand through his dark hair. "You may be right. Not every Aquillan cares for friendship with Earth. But don't forget, there were forty, maybe fifty or more of my people working in *SeaGlobe* when it was stolen. They're either all in this conspiracy, or they're just as much prisoners as every shark, mullet, and shellfish in the place."

"A good point," Admiral Silmon said, nodding affably at K'orlii. "I agree with you, son. Either someone's trying real hard to make Aquilla look bad—or your whole world has suddenly declared war on the Inner Planets. If they have, no one's bothered to tell *me* about it!"

The young people left Silmon's office to get into warmer clothes. Before Tom walked out the door, the officer took him aside. "I have a high-priority message from your father. He wants you to call him. I was about to send for you when this business on *SeaGlobe* happened. Why don't we meet here after you talk to him?"

"Will do. And thanks, Admiral." Tom raced to his room, changed, then hurried to Com Center. After a long conversation with Mr. Swift via deepspace radio, he met his companions back at Silmon's office.

"My father has asked us to go to the Swift

Enterprises installation on the Moon immediately," he announced.

Anita looked puzzled. "Did he say what for?"

"No. He didn't want to talk much, even over
the guarded channel. But from the tone of his
voice it's obvious that there's trouble."

"I'll give you an escort," Silmon said. "No use
taking any chances."

"I'd rather do without, sir." Tom said. "The
more company we have, the more attention we'll
likely attract. It's a short hop, and I don't think
we'll run into any trouble."

Silmon pondered that a moment. "I'll go along
with that though I'm not too sure it's a good idea.
We'll track tight, and the Lunar States patrols will
pick you up halfway." He turned and held out a
hand to K'orlii. "This business will get all cleared
up. Don't let it get to you."

"Thank you, sir," the Aquillan said, returning
the officer's grip. He smiled, but Tom could read
the concern in his gold-flecked eyes.

Repairs had been hurried on the *Exedra*, and
the techs at *New America* had done a first-class job
of putting the ship back together. At Tom's
instructions, no one had touched the shadowlator. Getting that back into shape was something
he'd have to handle himself.

After a thorough inflight check of all systems,

the young inventor turned the controls over to Aristotle. Then he picked up a report on the malfunction of the ship that Admiral Silmon had handed to him before they left the space colony.

He looked through it, then passed it to Ben. The computer expert read no further than the first page and gave a sharp whistle.

"Simple, huh?" Tom asked. "If you know how to do it."

"Right. And someone obviously did. Stuck one little microchip where it didn't belong." Ben groaned and ran a hand over his face. "Tom, no wonder we had a power overload. I'm surprised we didn't blow up the whole ship. We've got a real pro on our hands."

"Uh-huh. If you look at the last page you'll see that ex-employee of Swift Enterprises who suddenly disappeared is a near genius in two or three fields—including computer technology and electronic engineering."

"Great." Ben shook his head in disgust. "How do you suppose someone like that got mixed up with a bunch of crooks? He sure didn't *have* to." Ben squinted at the page. "This Edward Gatterby's got enough on the ball to start his own company."

Anita had poked her head into the cabin. "Maybe David Luna made him an offer he felt was too good to refuse," she said.

"Luna's dead," Ben grumbled.

"Someone like Luna, then?"

"There *is* no one else like Luna!"

Tom was catching a nap in his bunk on the afterdeck when the shrill clang of the *Exedra*'s alarm brought him up straight. By the time he got forward, Ben was already crouched over Aristotle's shoulder, peering intently into the scope.

"Take a look at this." Ben stood aside to let him through. Two green blips paced the *Exedra* to port. After a few moments, Tom saw they were holding their course a good 800 miles away. No closer, no further.

"Curious little devils, aren't they?" Tom said sourly.

"Perhaps we should have taken Admiral Silmon's offer of an escort," K'orlii spoke up behind him.

"Doesn't look like they want anything." Tom snapped on the com, punched in a Lunar States frequency, and plucked a headset off the wall. "Lunar Command, this is the *Exedra*. You monitoring traffic in our sector?"

"We have them," the crisp voice said immediately. "Two unauthorized craft. We're checking 'em out now. Advise you hold present course."

"Check. Thanks, Lunar Command." Tom

flipped off the switch and glanced at the scope. Almost instantly, the two blips accelerated and disappeared from the screen. A grin crossed Tom's features. Four Lunar ships appeared at the edge of the picture coming in fast.

"Looks like our friends don't want any company," he said.

Anita bristled. "Just what do you suppose they were *doing* here in the first place?"

"You want to know what I think?" Tom said evenly. "I don't think they wanted a thing. Except to let us know they haven't forgotten us."

Thunder died in the *Exedra*'s engines and the ship settled gently on the flat, oval plain in Copernicus Crater. The carrier shuttle bounced toward them on its outsized donut tires, and a moment later Tom heard the lock click into place on the ship's hull. The shuttle took them swiftly to Portal D, and Tom had only a glimpse of the lunar surface through the overhead port. The ghost-white rim of Copernicus was outlined sharply against the darkness of space.

Tom had expected Swift Enterprises executive Gene Larson to meet his party, but he was unprepared for the group of men that were with him. They looked decidedly unfriendly. Earth's Interplanet representative Henry Greylock was on hand, a red-faced man with a flaring white mustache and piercing eyes. Looming beside him was the gaunt, hawk-faced Marcus Overmann, Interplanet Councilor from the Lunar States. The other four men were tall, gray-uniformed members of the Lunar States Guard.

Marcus Overmann glared at Tom, then stalked right past him, and pointed a shaky finger at K'orlii. "Guards," he blurted, "he's the one right there, the Aquillan. Arrest him, and hold him under my personal custody!"

K'orlii stepped back a pace and stared at Overmann. Tom walked up and said, "Sir, I don't know what's going on here. Arrest him for *what*?"

Overmann's eyes narrowed. "Swift, this is no concern of yours. I advise you to mind your own business."

"Ah, Marcus," Greylock said amiably, "perhaps you're acting a little too hastily."

"Hastily?" Overmann turned on the representative from Earth. "Henry, this—this—young man here is a spy! An *enemy* agent. I do not intend to have him running about loose on the Moon!"

"K'orlii is no more an enemy agent than I am," said Tom. "Aquilla is an ally of Earth."

Overmann laughed out loud. "We know what happened on *New America*. It is not going to happen here, I assure you." He turned irritably to the guards. "Go on, men. Arrest him. We're wasting valuable time."

Two guards moved up beside K'orlii and grabbed his arms. K'orlii jerked away. "You have no right to do this!" he protested.

"Yes, he does," Tom said. "He has every right in the world, K'orlii."

"Tom!" Anita looked appalled. "Tom Swift, how can you just stand there and not *do* anything!" she said furiously.

"Take it easy," Tom told her. "He does have a right to arrest K'orlii. And of course, K'orlii has rights, too. Mister Larson—" Tom turned to the Swift Enterprises representative. "Would you please get in touch with my father on Earth? Tell him K'orlii would like to sue Mister Marcus Overmann for slander, false arrest, harassment—"

Overmann's eyes bulged. "Why, you can't do that! It's preposterous!"

"Yes, sir," Tom said politely, "I certainly can. And you can fight Swift Enterprises in court. And, Mister Larson, you might advise the Aquillan Consulate on the Moon and the embassy on Earth that Mister Overmann of the Lunar States has taken one of their citizens into custody on the charge of espionage. That he has stated, before several witnesses, that Aquilla is an enemy of Earth."

"I—never said any such thing!" Overmann spluttered. His hands curled into fists and trembled by his sides.

"Afraid you did." Greylock sighed.

"Huh?" Overmann turned on the man. "You agree to this, Henry? The boy's dangerous!"

"He may well be, Marcus. But I—ah—under the circumstances, I think we've bitten off a bit more than we can chew."

Overmann's face turned a bright shade of crimson. "I am not finished with you," he warned K'orlii. "Or you, either, Tom Swift! Just watch yourself while you are in the Lunar States!" Overmann turned and stalked angrily out of the lock. The guards followed. Henry Greylock shook his head and strode out after them.

"Okay," Anita said contritely. "I owe you one, friend."

"I kind of figured he was bluffing." Tom grinned. "I've run into Mister Overmann before. He didn't have a leg to stand on, and he knew it."

Gene Larson shook Tom's hand. "Glad to see that you gave it to the old boy." He chuckled. "Overmann asked for it. He usually does. Would've stepped in myself if you hadn't done such a good job."

"Overmann has his rights. But so does everyone else. He just hasn't figured that out yet."

Larson's big grin faded. "The only thing is, Tom, I'm afraid he's got plenty of reasons to be upset. That's why your dad wanted you to be on hand when he gets here. You see, we have more trouble than we can handle on the Moon!"

Chapter Seven

Gene Larson was Mr. Swift's chief assistant and Tom trusted him completely. He was a big man with deep, blue eyes and a brusque, straightforward manner. He was now leading Tom and his party through the fast tubeway system that ran under Copernicus Crater to the Swift Enterprises compound, and ushered them into a small conference room. Then he walked quickly to a squat metal box implanted in the far curve of the wall.

"Have to be careful these days," he grumbled. "That instrument's a security device. Had trouble with eavesdroppers here the last few weeks."

Tom frowned. "You mean, someone's bugging Swift Enterprises?"

"Right. We've found half a dozen microreceivers. Good ones, too. In the labs, conference rooms—even in my office."

Tom and Ben Walking Eagle exchanged a quick look.

"I know what you're thinking," Larson said, "and you're right. After the incidents in Triton dome, we went over the installation from top to bottom. Didn't find a thing. It was only when we discovered the bugs here that we checked Triton again. You were in *New America*, and haven't had time to see this."

He leaned over and touched a flat console on the table. The lights dimmed and a screen slid out of the wall. "Take a look," Larson said. "It'll give you an idea what we're up against."

At first, Tom thought a fly had landed on the screen. Then he realized the fly was the object that had been filmed. The camera zoomed in and the fly became larger, until it filled the entire screen. Tom could clearly see its wings, legs, and multifaceted eyes.

Suddenly, he sat up straight and stared. "I'm not sure I believe that!" he exclaimed.

"Me, neither," Ben echoed.

"That's how we reacted, too," Larson said. "It's true, though. That fly there, or the thing that looks like a fly, is an ultrasophisticated listening device."

He stood up and walked to the screen. "Of course, microminiaturization is nothing new—especially in the eavesdropping business. But the *technology* behind this little gadget gives you some idea of the outfit that's behind all this."

Tom studied the bright picture intently. Having a great deal of respect for the privacy of others, he was angered by what he saw. Yet, as an inventor, he couldn't help but marvel at the ingenious way the "fly" had been put together. It was a receiver, transmitter, relay point—a whole broadcasting station. And highly mobile, at that. In addition, it could not be called simply a *listening* device, as the large eyes contained sophisticated video equipment.

Ben was awed. "Fantastic, huh?"

"Fantastic doesn't cover it," Tom muttered. He turned to Anita. "You're a micro expert. Who do you know that could come up with something like this?"

"No one," Anita answered instantly. "No, wait. I take that back. Plenty of people could. *I* could, I guess. And so could you. All you'd need is unlimited money, highly trained people, and the very finest equipment available."

Tom let out a breath. "In other words, just about anyone could do it, *if* they had an organization like Swift Enterprises behind them."

Gene Larson pressed his lips together and

nodded. "Well, it wasn't us," he said flatly. "And that doesn't leave too many others. Marcus Overmann gets my vote."

"Wait a minute, now." Tom held up a hand. He knew what was going through Larson's mind. Besides his position as Interplanet Councilor from the Lunar States, Marcus Overmann was also president of the huge Luna Corporation, a post he'd assumed after the disappearance of David Luna.

"Mr. Overmann's a bad-tempered, pretty unlikable person," said Tom. "But that doesn't make him a crook."

"It gives him a good head start," Anita said drily.

"How about Henry Greylock?" Ben suggested. "He's not exactly running a hole-in-the-wall shop anymore either."

Tom agreed. Greylock's business had grown rapidly in a very short time, until he was almost as tough a competitor of Swift Enterprises as the Luna Corporation. Still, Tom had always found the man fair-minded, and knew that his father thought so as well.

"Maybe they're both in it together," Larson suggested.

"Ganging up on Swift Enterprises?" Tom asked.

Larson shrugged. "It's not impossible."

Tom stood up and paced the room. "We're doing the same thing Marcus Overmann tried to do to K'orlii. Accusing him of things we can't prove. Besides, who else is on our list?" Tom stopped and marked them off quickly on his fingers. "A couple of other big companies in the Inner Planets. The Aquillans, maybe. Sorry, K'orlii, but we have to consider that. Maybe the Asteroid Confederation. That's about it."

"Well, there are a couple of other things you ought to know, as long as we're playing guessing games," Larson added. "Remember I told you we had troubles here on the Moon? I wasn't just talking about TV stations that crawl up the wall and look like flies."

"There's more?" Tom frowned.

"Afraid so. That's why I said Overmann's got some right to be upset. There was an explosion in one of the Luna Corporation's locks not ten hours ago that blew out a whole portal and scattered stuff all over the floor of the crater. Fortunately, there was only freight in there at the time, and no one was hurt. About an hour after that, someone played a real cute trick with the main air-supply system." Larson's face looked grim. "If a tech hadn't caught the problem in time, a couple of hundred people might have found themselves real short of breath."

Tom's face flushed with anger. "Mister Larson—

whoever these people are, it seems they'll stop at nothing to get what they want!"

"Which is what?" Anita asked. "We never have come up with an answer to that."

"We know they stole *SeaGlobe*," K'orlii said gloomily.

"But we haven't the slightest idea why," Tom reminded him.

"Well—" Gene Larson pulled his stout frame erect and looked at Tom. "While you're thinking on all that, I've saved one unpleasant little surprise for the last."

"I can't imagine what you left out," Tom said darkly.

"You will when you see it," Larson said bluntly. "Come on, we have to get to this sooner or later."

Tom stormed through the ruins of his lab, trying hard to control his temper. Someone had tossed a firebomb into the room, closed the door, and left. The bomb had generated such an intense heat that half the lab was blackened before the fire safety system could blanket the room with foam.

"Just look at it," Tom raged. "Ben, they weren't after anything. There was no purpose in this except to destroy everything in sight."

"And let *you* know they could do it," sighed

Anita. She perched on the edge of an undamaged worktable. "It was a warning, Tom. Pure and simple. They thumbed their noses at you and said, 'See—we can get away with anything we want!' "

"You're right I'm afraid," Tom said glumly.

"I know I am." Anita turned to Aristotle. "Have you figured out how they got past the fingerprint lock? I thought that was supposed to be impossible."

"Yes, Anita, it is. Whoever is responsible for the intense combustion in this area did not enter the room at all. Tom's fingerprint lock is intact, and has not been disturbed."

"What?" Tom sat up straight. "Then how *did* they get in?"

Aristotle raised a slim metal finger and stabbed at the wall. "Through that, Tom. The air-conditioning vent."

Tom shook his head. "Too small. Nothing that's more than a quarter-inch wide could get through there."

"A quarter-inch is fairly accurate," Aristotle droned. "The object that entered the room was a wasp."

"A what?" Tom looked intently at the robot.

"A wasp," Aristotle repeated. "A wasp is a winged insect belonging chiefly to the family

Vespidae, and the order *Hymenoptera*. They—"

"Aristotle, I *know* what a wasp is," Tom said impatiently. "Would you kindly explain what you're talking about?"

"Certainly, Tom. The insect I am speaking of is not truly an insect at all, but a man-made imitation. In one sense, a robot like myself, though not nearly so complex or finely attuned to its environment . . ."

"Yes, Aristotle. Get on with it, please."

"The fire was started by electronic wasps. Several dozen, I would imagine. Each, of course, was a miniature firebomb."

Tom scratched his head. "How do you know that for sure? Nothing could have survived this fire."

"Correction. Nothing could have lasted if it had been *caught* in the fire." Aristotle walked up to Tom. A small utility drawer snapped open in his chest. The robot lifted out an object with his stainless steel fingers and handed it to Tom.

Tom squinted and almost dropped it. "Good grief, what if this thing decides to go off!"

"It will not," Aristotle assured him. "It was defective to begin with, and I have further defused it."

Ben, Anita, and K'orlii gathered around to peer at the tiny jeweled insect in Tom's hand.

"It's fantastic," Anita said under her breath. "Absolutely fantastic!"

"And deadly," Tom added grimly. He looked up at the robot. "When did you find this?"

"When we entered the laboratory, Tom. Twenty-nine and one-half minutes ago."

"Well, why didn't you say something?"

"You didn't ask," Aristotle said simply.

Tom Swift made no effort to clean up the section of his laboratory destroyed by the fire. There was nothing to be done; everything was burned to a crisp. Instead, he spent his time devising a makeshift electronic field that would effectively bar any further metal bugs from entering the lab.

Finally, he rummaged around his workbench and brought out a flat piece of metal and a small plastic box.

"Here's something you haven't seen before," he said to his friends.

Ben looked at the object curiously. "What is it? Doesn't look like much."

"Come now, you know an awful lot can be packed into a small package these days!"

"Like receiving stations and firebombs," K'orlii reminded him.

"Okay." Ben held up his hands in surrender. "I'm outnumbered. I'll sit down and shut up."

Anita rolled her eyes. "I wish I had a camera to record this moment. Ben Walking Eagle shuts up."

Tom laughed. "As a matter of fact, the moment *is* recorded, Anita. Watch."

His fingers moved hurriedly over the surface of the device in his hand. Suddenly, the ruined end of the lab disappeared. In its place was a vivid, three-dimensional copy of the scene that had taken place only moments before.

"*. . . Like receiving stations and firebombs.*"

"*Okay. I'm outnumbered. I'll sit down and shut up.*"

"*I wish I had a camera to record this moment. Ben Walking Eagle shuts up.*"

"*As a matter of fact, the moment* is *recorded, Anita. Watch. . . .*"

Tom clicked off the device. Abruptly, the scene vanished.

"A holographic receiver *and* a projector," Anita exclaimed. "Now when did you find time to come up with *that*?"

"I've had it stewing for a while," Tom said.

"But—how did you get all of that out of one small package?" Ben shook his head. "That is a real accomplishment, friend."

"Not nearly as big a deal as micro-firebombs," Tom said. "But a whole lot safer. Actually, three-dimensional laser photography is nothing new.

I've just managed to package the system in a convenient size, and add a few refinements of my own."

"Such as?" prompted Ben.

"Well, sound *and* smell, for instance."

Ben grinned. "We've had smell in entertainment units for years, Tom."

Tom laughed. "Not like this you haven't. My holoprojector goes a couple of steps further. Look." He held up the smaller of the two packages and slid it open. It was the shape of a matchbox, and contained fingernail-sized holographic microcassettes. "Let's try this one." He inserted a tiny cassette in the metal instrument, then pressed three buttons on the top.

The others gasped and nearly jumped out of their chairs. The corner of the room was suddenly a dark, angry sea. Wind lashed at the enormous, foam-flecked waves and sent them rolling over the trio with a deafening roar. The smell of cold salt spray filled the air. Lightning and thunder ripped the sky overhead. A giant, rolling crest swelled on the horizon and grew until it engulfed everything in sight. The monster loomed over them all for an awesome moment, then crashed with a terrible fury.

Tom pressed a button and the scene vanished.

"Wow!" Anita swallowed hard and gave him a

withering look. "Tom Swift, the next time I want to be entertained, I'll let you know. Okay?"

"Pretty realistic, isn't it?"

Ben ran a hand through his hair. "Yeah, that's one thing you could call it. Realistic."

"The image for all of that is on one tiny chip of film?" K'orlii asked.

"Right." Tom clicked the storm scene out of the holoprojector and slipped it back in the box. "So far, I've got a fair little collection. Hurricanes, volcanic eruptions, a ride through the rings of Saturn."

"Anything quiet and peaceful?" Anita asked warily.

"How about a sunset over the Grand Canyon?"

"I think that's about my speed," Anita admitted. "I've been getting all the real, genuine excitement I can use lately!"

Tom and the boys left Anita in the hall and walked toward their room to change for dinner. Tom wondered whether his father had arrived yet and thought about checking with Gene Larson. But then he decided against it. He'd be told as soon as Mr. Swift had landed.

Ben sensed his thoughts. "What do you think this business is—"

Suddenly, Aristotle, who had been walking

ahead of them, stopped and faced Tom. "I must inform you that I have been probing ahead toward your sleeping quarters," he said quietly. "I can tell you that I have already discovered at least three listening and viewing devices implanted there. . . ."

Chapter Eight

Tom looked at the robot. "Are you sure of that? They've already got bugs in our rooms?"

"Is that a question, Tom? Your use of the word 'sure' seems to indicate re-evaluation of my data. I am doing this now, and I will—"

"Forget it, Aristotle." Tom waved the robot's question aside. "That's not what I meant at all."

"Well, I know what *I'm* going to do," Ben said tightly. "This is the last straw, Tom. I say we dig out every phony housefly, wasp, or whatever they've got buzzin' around in there and swat 'em back into steel shavings!"

"Ben, hold it." Tom reached out and pulled his friend back. I've got a better idea."

"Such as?"

"Let's not do anything."

"Huh?" Ben gave him a blank look. "You mean just let them get away with this?"

"Right. Maybe we'll tell those little electronic pets something we *want* them to hear."

K'orlii grinned, and Ben said, "Okay. I know what you're thinking. But I still don't like the idea of silver bugs flying around in my room."

Before Tom went to sleep, he sent Aristotle to check Anita's quarters for bugs. When he returned, he gave Tom a signal with his stainless steel hand and nodded. Tom wasn't surprised. He went to bed and slept uneasily.

It was Ben's idea to work out before breakfast. The only exercise they'd had recently was anything but voluntary, and they were eager to get the kinks out of their muscles.

Swift Enterprises maintained a gym that could be adjusted to simulate the surface gravity of Earth, but most visitors were delighted to work out under lunar conditions. At one-sixth their regular weight, even the clumsiest people became instant Olympic champions.

The gym looked nothing like gyms found on Earth. It was an enormous room lasered out of sublunarian rock. The big, square-shaped cavern measured thirty yards in every direction. Strong, elastic netting covered the walls, floors, and ceiling, giving the overall effect of a great cage.

At such an early morning hour, Tom and his friends had the place to themselves. They entered at the mid-level lock, forty-five feet above the floor. Tom and Ben, who suddenly weighed only about twenty-seven pounds apiece, pushed off from the wall, doubled up, and did matching quadruple somersaults to the far side of the gym. Bracing their knees for a landing, they pushed off hard, gained extra speed from the spring of the net, and looped out over the gym in super-slow swan dives.

Anita and K'orlii passed them in mid-air, shooting like missiles for the ceiling. Then Anita came down from a complicated routine that involved timing her trajectory to hit the exact center of each of the gym's six planes. It was a great deal like bouncing around inside a trampoline square.

"You're not bad," Tom taunted the girl, "for a one-legged acrobat."

"Huh!" She raised her chin and finished lacing her shoe up tight. "Anytime, Tom Swift, I'll run you ragged around this place and leave you with your tongue hanging out."

Tom laughed. "You can do it, too. I've got

more sense than to take up your challenge." He bounced off the net and pushed himself to the floor underneath where his robot stood watching. "Aristotle, you ought to join us up there. Work all the rust out of your joints."

Aristotle's lavender electric eyes peered at Tom. "Is that an order or a suggestion?" he asked.

"Neither, Aristotle. Just a comment, really."

"Good," Aristotle said flatly. "I really see no logical way in which I would benefit from such an experience. The physical muscle tone of a human in no way approximates that of the structure of—"

"All right!" Tom held two palms up to the robot. "Forget it!"

Anita laughed, and looked up to watch Ben and K'orlii playing a lunar version of football. It wasn't an easy task under light-gravity conditions. K'orlii pushed off from the far side of the wall, a good seventy feet from the floor. Ben watched him, cocked his right arm, and let go. K'orlii and the football came together perfectly, though the action seemed to take all day. It looked to Tom like slow-motion replay of a game on Earth.

K'orlii tossed the ball back to Ben, and Anita rushed him from below. Ben, startled to find her streaking toward him, threw the ball too quickly. K'orlii yelled and stretched for it. Tom hit him with a lazy, mid-air tackle that set them both spinning toward the far wall. The ball jerked free and tumbled slowly to the floor of the gym, moving with all the speed of a rock dropping through heavy syrup.

Twenty minutes later, all four were sprawled out exhausted in the lower net. "You know what?" Tom rubbed a towel over his face and let out a breath. "We are flat out of shape, gang. A month ago, we could have kept that up for an hour."

"You're right," Anita groaned. "I'm beat. Totally."

"You missed a great many passes today," K'orlii said. "That is not like you at all, Ben."

"What?" Ben sat up and thrust out his chin. "Hey, come *on*, *you* were short. I was right there."

"You were nearly as bad as Tom." Anita laughed.

"Okay. So I wasn't up to par. I admit it. None of us were."

It was true, and Tom couldn't imagine why. He turned over on his back, picked up the ball, and tossed it idly in the air. The pigskin came down faster than he'd figured and hit him in the chest. He looked curiously at the football, then tossed it again. This time he caught it perfectly. "Listen," he said, the humor suddenly gone from his voice, "it's not me, or any of us. It's the gym. There's something wrong in here."

Ben pulled himself up and bounced on the net. "You're right. Gravity's different. It sure isn't point-one-six. Not by a long shot."

"Aristotle," Tom snapped, "give me a reading."

"Zero-point-three-nine," the robot answered.

"I thought so!" Tom sprang from the net to the floor. "We're not losing our touch, there's a malfunction in the gravitic equipment. We're heavier than we were."

"Tom—that reading was accurate when you asked," the robot droned. "Now the gravity of this room, relative to a standard one-point-zero on Earth, is zero-point-six-two and rising."

"I don't like this," Ben said stiffly.

"I don't either. Not one bit." Tom made his way to the door on the ground level. When his hands gripped the heavy bar mechanism, a chill ran down his spine. "Locked!" he shouted. "We're trapped in here!"

Ben, K'orlii, and Anita spilled out of the net and joined him. "Give me a running report," Ben instructed the robot, "every time there's a change."

"It is changing now," Aristotle answered. "Zero-point-nine-seven."

"I can feel it!" gasped Anita. She stared at Tom. "We're nearly back to our normal weight. If it goes on from there—"

"Right, said Tom, tension straining his voice. "And I have a good idea it isn't going to stop. Ben, K'orlii—give me a hand with this door!"

The two helped Tom push with all their strength. The horizontal bar seemed welded solid to the lock. Ben stood back and shook his head. "No good, Tom. That's a pressure door. We'll never budge it."

"We *have* to," Tom said tightly. "Someone's playing with the gravity in here."

"One-point-one-seven . . . point-one-nine," Aristotle reported.

"We're already heavier than we are on Earth," Ben said.

"Aristotle, get over here," Tom ordered. He measured the door with his eyes. "The lock mechanism ought to be about—there. Hit it with a tight laser beam. Full utility power."

The robot held a stainless steel palm inches from the metal surface. A beam of intense red light bored into the door. A circle the size of a coin began to glow, turn cherry-red then white.

"Keep it going," Tom urged the robot. "Don't stop, Aristotle."

"Tom," Anita said anxiously, "I can feel the drag. Every muscle in my body's beginning to sag."

Tom felt it, too. His legs were as heavy as lead. "Gravity, Aristotle. What is it now?"

"One-point-seven-five, Tom."

"No wonder I feel lousy," Ben complained. "I weigh almost—three hundred pounds!"

Anita gripped the wall, then slid to the ground, too exhausted to get up.

"Don't try," Tom warned her. "Stay there and save your strength. Aristotle—don't stop. Keep that laser going!"

"Continual use of the laser is draining my power, Tom. I am using a great deal of energy just to stay on my feet. The gravity pull is two-point-zero. I weigh just under a thousand pounds, now. I was not built for this."

"You can't stop," gasped Tom. "Got to—get through that door . . ."

Ben and K'orlii sank to the floor. Tom tried to hold out but couldn't. He sagged to the ground and lay flat, sucking in great breaths of air. His heart beat wildly against his chest. His normal, hard-muscled 170-pound body was approaching 350 . . . 375. Tom had sustained greater G-forces during rocket thrusts in space, but only for short periods of time. And there had been gravity suits to ease the pressure on the vital organs of the body. Now there was no protection against this force. If the gravity kept increasing, they would be crushed to death in a few minutes!

"*Arrrriss—tot—uhhhl . . .*" Tom's lips were drawn back over his teeth. He couldn't guess what the pressure was now.

"I am abandoning the laser, Tom . . ."

"*Noooooo!*"

"I must, Tom. I am switching to—mechanical —*eeeerk!*—power now. Using the—diamond dr*eeeeek!*—drill. It is all I can do. I can barely move as it is. My—*aaaaaak!*—circuits are snapping under the pressure."

Tom's vision was only a blur. Aristotle struggled somewhere above him. The high whine of the drill fell into silence. The robot strained against the terrible pull of gravity. Again and again, he threw his great strength against the door. His fists and shoulders ground metal. Something cracked and gave way. Tom, nearly unconscious now, couldn't tell whether it was Aristotle or the door. Then, everything around him went black.

"Tom! Tom, are you all right?"

Tom opened his eyes and looked up into the anxious face of Gene Larson. Relief crossed Larson's features and he helped Tom to his feet.

Swift Enterprise guards and medical personnel were giving a hand to K'orlii, Ben, and Anita. Tom tried to stand by himself and nearly fell on his face.

"Easy now," warned Larson.

"The rest of you okay?" Tom said weakly.

"Guess so," said Ben. "Don't think we need any more exercise today, though."

Larson's features were grim. "That robot of yours almost tore a solid steel door off its hinges." He shook his head in wonder. "Good thing, too. Besides tampering with the gravity in here, someone conveniently shorted out the alarm system as well. We would never have known what happened until it was too late."

"Good old Aristotle," said Tom. "Is he all right?"

"I am not in perfect condition," Aristotle droned. "However, I am analyzing my damage and repairing circuits quickly."

"Great. And thanks, Aristotle. We owe you one, for sure."

"If I was employed under some system of merit, Tom, perhaps this would be so. However—"

"Never mind." Tom laughed. "We're grateful anyway." He stretched sore muscles and joined the others. "Anyone feel like breakfast?"

Anita was horrified. "Are you kidding? After gaining about three hundred pounds in five minutes, I'm going on a *very* strict diet, Tom Swift."

Gene Larson joined them at breakfast. The infirmary had given them a clean bill of health and declared them well enough to down a large-sized meal.

"I'll say one thing," Anita exclaimed firmly, "hanging out with you guys is *not* boring."

"Boredom is something I'd welcome right now," Tom mused. "About twenty-four hours of doing nothing would be fine."

Just then, a Swift Enterprises guard burst into the room. His eyes were wide, and his skin was pasty-white.

"Sir," he blurted, "someone just broke into Mister Greylock's room and shot him with a laser!"

Chapter Nine

Henry Greylock was still very much alive. He had jumped aside at the last moment, and the laser had only creased the top of his shoulder.

"Overmann started the rumor that Earth's Interplanet Councilor was dead. The news services spread it all over the system before they found out it wasn't true," Gene Larson said. "He also said an Aquillan did it."

"So everyone is mad at Aquilla," K'orlii said. "How can this be, when none of it is true?"

"I'm afraid that part *is* true," Larson said reluctantly. "Greylock and two of his people swear they saw this hooded intruder, and that he was definitely an Aquillan."

Tom sighed. The damage was done. Overmann had what he wanted. He'd even turned the incident in the gym to his advantage. The story came out as another "Aquillan plot," and conveniently ignored the fact that K'orlii, a native of that planet, had also been trapped in the room.

"I cannot *stand* that man," fumed Anita. "Tom, he doesn't care what the truth is, if it doesn't match *his* version of the story."

By mid-afternoon, Aquillan representatives were ready to cut off friendly relations with the Earth, the Moon, and everyone else in the system. Tom cornered Marcus Overmann in his office. He wasn't surprised to find Henry Greylock there, his arm in a sling.

Overmann looked up as Tom burst in. "What are you doing here?" he said crossly. "I have nothing to say to you!"

"Yes, sir," said Tom. "I know that, but I'd appreciate it if you'd just listen a minute."

'Whatever it is, I don't care to hear it."

"Now, Marcus—" Henry Greylock brushed his flowing white mustache. "Don't be so all-fired stubborn. Won't hurt to hear what the boy has to say." He gave Tom an encouraging nod.

"Thank you, sir," said Tom. "I hope you're feeling better, Mister Councilor."

"I'm fine," said Greylock. "My, ah, wounding was somewhat exaggerated."

"Hmmmph!" Overmann's hawkish features tightened in a scowl. "Looks to me like you ought to start figuring out who your *friends* are, Henry. It sure isn't Swift Enterprises or those Aquillans. If someone took a shot at *me*, I think I'd wake up and take a good long look at who was pulling the trigger!"

"Marcus," Greylock said patiently, "we have been over this a hundred times—"

"If you don't mind my saying so," Tom interrupted, "there's something you're forgetting, Mister Overmann."

"Eh? And what might that be?"

"Just why Swift Enterprises or Aquilla would want to cause all this trouble. No one has anything to gain by it. Friendly relations with the star worlds have always led to better trade, and scientific advancement. What good would it do us to tear all that down?"

Overman's mouth curled into a sly grin. "You don't think I see it, do you?"

"See—what, sir?"

"What you and your father are up to!" Overmann's face turned scarlet and his fists slammed the table in a rage. "This whole thing is a plot to put the Luna Corporation out of business. But you won't get away with it—I'll tell you that for certain!"

Tom was totally bewildered at the man's outburst. "Mister Overmann—"

"Get out," Overmann screamed. "Get *out* of this office, Swift, and don't come back!"

A short time later, Tom and his friends were halfway down the long hallway leading from Swift Enterprises' headquarters to their rooms near the edge of the compound.

"He's completely unreasonable," Tom complained. "I don't think he even knows why he's so angry. Mister Greylock's his friend, and he can't make him see the truth, either."

"I don't think Overmann *wants* to be reasonable," Anita said.

"It sure doesn't look like it," Tom conceded. Then he stopped suddenly, looked over his shoulder, and motioned the others to him. "Maybe we can't clear this business up, but we can give it a try," he said. "I don't imagine you've forgotten that our quarters are still bugged."

"Not likely." Ben frowned. "The whole idea gives me the creeps."

"With a little luck, perhaps we can give someone else the creeps!"

"What do you have in mind?" K'orlii asked.

"If they want to know what we're up to, why don't we tell 'em?" He took a scrap of paper out of his pocket and pressed it against the wall, then drew a quick sketch. He handed it to Ben. "You and Anita rig up something like this. Then meet us in Corridor L."

Ben grinned. "Be glad to. We'll be ready in half an hour."

Corridor L was small and narrow and led to the gymnasium where Tom and his friends had nearly been crushed to death earlier. Now, the four crouched in a dark utility closet just outside the gym door. The closet was small and stuffy, not meant for people to sit in.

"Maybe it's not going to work," Anita whispered. "How long have we been in this thing?"

"It'll work," said Tom. "Just give it time." He glanced at the glowing digits on his watch. "We've only been here—forty-nine minutes."

"Seem's long enough." K'orlii sighed.

Tom was concerned himself, but tried not to show it. He was certain the conversation he and K'orlii had faked in their room was clear. If someone didn't bite on that . . .

"Hey, hold it!" Ben grabbed Tom's arm. "I'm getting something." He snapped on a penlight and aimed it at the small meter in his palm. The thin black needle quivered slightly, jerking from side to side!

"He's in there," Ben whispered. "He's walking now . . . see how the needle's moving? He—" Ben almost yelled as the needle jumped violently to the right. "Come on, we've got him!"

They dashed out of the closet and raced to the lock in front of the gym. Slamming the bar-latch aside, Tom burst into the room and instinctively threw himself aside. But then he saw there was no need for caution. The intruder was swinging upside down, halfway to the high ceiling. He was yelling and thrashing about, but there was no way he could loose himself from the tangle of nets that held him like a fish.

Anita gazed up, hands on her hips, and nodded with satisfaction. "What do you suppose we've caught here, Ben?"

"I don't know," Ben told her, "but whatever it is, I'm going to keep it."

"What we ought to do is just leave him right there. Turn up the Gees to about *ten* and see what happens."

"You wouldn't do that!" the prisoner cried fearfully.

"You're right," said Anita. "We wouldn't. Not everybody thinks like you do."

Tom turned at the clatter of boots in the hall and saw Marcus Overmann and a dozen Lunar Guardsmen. The gaunt councilor froze in his tracks at the sight.

"Wh-what is the meaning of all this? Who is that man and what is he doing up there?"

"I don't know who he is," Tom said calmly. "You'll have to ask him. I *do* know what he's doing up there. He overheard K'orlii and me talking about a piece of evidence we'd hidden behind the netting on the wall. Guess he just couldn't wait to find it."

A tall Lunar Guard captain with sharp features turned to Tom. "What kind of evidence?"

"There wasn't any. This fellow figured whatever he heard over his bugs that he planted in our rooms must be true."

The captain smiled slightly. Marcus Overmann looked annoyed.

The prisoner was down now and on his feet, surrounded by gray-clad officers. "Who are you?" Overmann demanded. "You have a name, sir?"

The man glared bleakly but said nothing.

"Well, you'll talk. I am certain of that." Thrusting out his jaw, Overmann stalked out of the room past Tom and the others.

Tom studied the intruder, and had the feeling he'd seen him before.

"Captain," he asked, "if it's all the same to you, we'd like to follow through on this."

The captain chewed his lip a moment. "You can come up to headquarters if you like," he said.

"Can't promise more than that. This fellow's got a right to a hearing. Or to keep his mouth shut, if he wants to."

"My friends and I nearly got killed in this room," Tom said, trying to suppress his anger. "I'd like the people responsible for that to get what's coming to them."

"Yes, well. . . ." The captain ran a hand over his bristly jaw. "For your sake, friend, I hope he's one of them."

"What?" Tom looked perplexed. "Of course he's one of them!"

"So you say. All I know is, you and your friends set a trap in here and some guy stepped in it. Could be you're the ones in trouble, not him."

Tom followed the man, furious behind a calm exterior. "With our luck, that's exactly what'll happen," he grumbled. "That guy'll go free and we'll end up in a cell under the Moon."

The Lunar Guard captain, whose name was Kerrick, stepped out of his office and motioned to Tom and Ben. Anita and K'orlii had left twenty minutes before to see Gene Larson.

"Sorry to keep you waiting," the captain said. "Have a seat." Tom noticed he was a little friendlier than before, and wondered if that was good news or bad. Kerrick eased himself behind a desk and laced his hands behind his head.

"Well, the man denied everything," he announced. "Said he just went in there to work out in the gym."

"Of course he would!" Ben blurted.

"There's more," the captain went on, picking up a sheaf of notes and squinting at them. "We ran his name through I.D. Matches with his card. He *did* have a right to be there. He's a Swift Enterprises employee."

"He—is?" Tom's heart sank.

"Right. Name's John Gatterby. Tech Sixth Grade."

"Gatterby!" Tom jumped out of his chair and turned to Ben. "That guy who disappeared from Triton dome."

"Right," Ben said. "Edward Gatterby. Kind of a funny coincidence."

"Nope. Afraid not," Kerrick said. "That came out of the computer, too. John T. Gatterby is the brother of Edward R. Gatterby, a Swift employee who disappeared under questionable circumstances from Triton dome."

"Right." Tom felt suddenly weary. "I thought the guy looked familiar. You're going to hold him, aren't you, Captain? I'm certain he and his brother are both mixed up in this."

"Are you?" Kerrick raised a quizzical brow. "Then you know more than the Lunar Guards.

We don't have a thing but circumstantial evidence against Gatterby. And very little of that."

"But his brother—" Ben started.

"You don't go to jail because of your brother," Tom finished. "And we haven't really proven anything on *him*, either—"

Kerrick's door burst open and Gene Larson bounded in. He was fuming. "Captain Kerrick," he said bluntly, "I'm Larson. Swift Enterprises. We went through Gatterby's quarters soon as I got your call. Our security people found this." He tossed a small sack on the desk.

Kerrick turned it over and emptied it. "Well, now." A smile broadened his mouth. "Quite a little collection, Mister Larson. What are you folks running over there at Swift Enterprises?"

"Now look—" Larson began hotly.

"—pocket laser pistol. Illegal just about everywhere. Electronic lockpicks. Good set. What's this?" Kerrick pushed a transparent sack around on the table.

"Bugs. Listening devices," Larson said glumly.

"I'll take your word for it. Now here's a nice little item." The captain picked up a six-inch piece of intricately carved jade, studied it a moment, then firmly pressed its sides. Suddenly, the jade was tipped by a humming blur of silver.

"What—what in the world is *that* thing?" asked Larson.

"Vibrablade," Kerrick replied. "Razor-sharp and pulsing so fast you can hardly see it." He pressed the jade shaft again and the silvery motion disappeared. "Does a real nasty job on whatever it cuts. People, mostly." He stood up. "To answer your question, Tom, we'll be holding Gatterby, all right. Everything in this sack is a felony offense." He gave Larson a kindly grin. "Thanks for your help, friend."

Gene Larson brooded all the way back to his office. Tom knew what was bothering him and said nothing. When Larson was sprawled in his own chair again, he turned to Tom and let out a breath. "I got plenty upset when I learned this Gatterby was ours." Larson tapped his fingers on the desk. "Marcus Overmann is going to *love* this. Backs up all that nonsense he's been tossing out about Swift Enterprises and the Aquillans ganging up on the Luna Corporation. If that doesn't—"

Suddenly, a small red light started winking on the desk. Larson got out of the chair and bounded across the room.

"What—what is it?" gasped Tom.

"Your father's private office," Larson yelled over his shoulder. "*No* one can break in there, only someone just did!"

Chapter Ten

Larson was mad enough to chew nails. For him, this final intrusion was the last straw. He burst into the dimly lit room, his bulk filling the narrow frame of the door. A figure moved in the far corner, past a shadowy wall filled with books.

"All right," Larson warned, "hold it right there, mister!" A familiar chuckle came from the dark, then light flooded the room.

"Wha—!" Gene Larson blinked in astonishment. "Good grief, it's you!"

"Sorry, Gene, didn't mean to startle you." Tom's father stepped across the room and gripped Larson's hand. "Came in without any fuss so I could talk to you and Tom first. Well, good to see you, son!"

Tom walked up and shook his father's hand. "I should have known." He grinned. "There's no way to guess where you'll turn up."

Mr. Swift's smile matched his son's. "From what I've been hearing, it's a trait that runs in the family." He turned and greeted Anita, Ben, and K'orlii. Mr. Swift's eyes were a deep, startling blue. The leathery tan on his face contrasted sharply with the light, sandy hair touched with patches of iron gray at the temples.

Gene Larson and the young people took seats, while Tom's father perched on the edge of his desk and jammed his hands in his pockets. "I'm glad I caught you all together," he told them. "There's a lot to be done, and we don't have much time." His eyes flicked quickly about the room. Tom knew his father well and read his mood. There was tension in the elder Swift's manner.

Before Mr. Swift went further, Gene Larson filled him in on recent events—the incident in the gym, and the attempt on Henry Greylock's life. Mr. Swift's face clouded at the news. "I've known about the plot against *Ark Two* for some time," he said. "We've had hints of trouble before. Unfortunately, we didn't react fast enough. Our adversaries are bolder than we imagined. I don't have to tell you folks that. You already know what they're capable of doing."

"Mister Swift," Ben asked, "do you have any idea who it is we're up against?"

"No, I don't. Obviously, it's an extremely cunning and well-organized group. Their theft of *SeaGlobe* proved that. They've been one step ahead of us all the way."

"Do you believe some of my people are involved?" K'orlii asked.

"Yes, K'orlii, I think that is possible. But not in the way you may think," Mr. Swift added quickly. "You know your father and I have worked closely to bring our people together. We're still working, and we will continue those efforts."

He stood up abruptly. "I have a lot more to tell you, but I think it would be easier if you saw for yourselves." He grinned at the expression on their faces. "Hold the questions. You'll know a lot more in a minute."

With that, he led them past the long rows of bookcases to a solid oak panel and pressed a section of the grain. The panel slid noiselessly aside to reveal a small, six-by-six-foot elevator. Tom's father ushered them in, then let the panel close. A soft hum of power filled the small cubicle, followed by a subtle hint of movement.

Tom and Gene Larson knew where they were going, but the others were unprepared for the sight that awaited them. The elevator had stopped at a peak in the high, craggy rim sur-rounding Copernicus Crater. Everyone present had been in space before, and walked on other worlds. Still, there was something about the stark, cold beauty of Earth's own Moon that overwhelmed them. The transparent dome that covered the high perch curved clear to the smooth stone floor. There was nothing on any side but an endless view of the pocked lunar surface.

"There's not much you can say, is there?" Anita spoke in a small voice.

Tom's father smiled. "I call it my thinking room. Kind of gets me away from everything. This wasn't what I brought you here to see, though. Look. Up there. Straight overhead."

Tom turned his gaze. The starship *Daniel Boone* loomed high over Copernicus Crater, a crystal needle against a curtain of diamond-chip stars. The *Boone* always thrilled him, but there was more than the slender ship to see now.

"The domes," he said under his breath. "You've brought the domes here from *New America*!" Tom marveled at the sight, as did Anita and the others. They were all there, eight bright ecosystems circling the starship like miniature moons themselves: *KenyaWorld*, *Oasis/Sahara*, *SequoiaGreen*, and the rest.

"*SeaGlobe* should be there, too," Mr. Swift said, bitterness edging his voice. He offered them all soft, contoured chairs, but kept to his feet. "As I said, those devils outguessed us, whoever they are. We were on our way to get the domes, and they beat us by a matter of hours."

"Where are the ecosystems going now?" Larson asked.

"I've been planning on this a long time," the elder Swift replied. "We've been secretly outfitting the *Daniel Boone* for this special mission at one of our test stations past the orbit of Mars." He paused a moment to emphasize his words. "We are going to the star worlds, my friends."

"To the star worlds?" Anita asked. "Why, Mister Swift? It's not because of the attack of *New America*. You said this has been in the works for some time."

"It has," Tom's father explained. "The scientists who conceived the idea of removing Earth's endangered species to controlled environments felt from the beginning they'd have a far better chance of surviving in a natural atmosphere. Like Aquilla, with its vast, unpolluted seas. And Arborea IV—a whole, lush planet of thriving forests."

"And now there's another reason," Tom put in, "with the ecosystems in danger."

"Yes," Mr. Swift said flatly, pressing his hands

against the dome. "Someone intends to stop us. Why, I can't imagine. I will tell you this though. I will see to it that the *Daniel Boone* and its eight globes *will* reach the star worlds safely!" He paused, and turned to his listeners. "I want you all to come with us, and lend your expertise aboard the *Boone*. We'll be traveling with a very light crew. K'orlii, I think you'll be pleased to learn our first stop is Aquilla. Though I'm afraid we have nothing to deliver there for the moment."

K'orlii's face brightened. "It will be good to see my home again. And my family and friends as well."

"There's just one small hurdle we have to jump before we go," Mr. Swift added wryly. "The ecosystems project was completed under a grant from the Interplanet Council. We can't take it anywhere without their approval, and that means a vote."

"Seems to me like you already have." Larson grinned at the ceiling.

"You're right, Gene. I did that on my own. Sort of an emergency procedure, you might say."

"Dad, that won't be a small hurdle," Tom pointed out. "Marcus Overmann isn't exactly Swift Enterprises' biggest fan."

"I don't think he'd vote to toss you a rope if you were drowning," Larson growled.

Mr. Swift laughed. "I don't either. But

there's one thing you can always count on. Marcus will vote for *any*thing that makes him look good. And that's exactly the way I intend to present this to him!"

Tom saw little of his father or friends during the next few days, but there was plenty to keep him busy. Swift Enterprises' Earth and Moon facilities had gone into action around the clock to ferry the thousand and one items needed for the trip up to the *Daniel Boone*. Ben was pressed into service to iron out computer problems. Anita worked on the electronic systems that assured the health and well-being of the animals and plants housed in the eight globes tethered to the starship. K'orlii easily transferred his talents at managing sea creatures to handling the needs of land animals.

Tom worked closely with Gene Larson, trying to make sure everything that had to be done was accomplished in one way or the other.

One day Larson stalked across the floor of the bay and walked up to Tom and Anita. "You two probably haven't heard this," he said soberly.

"Now what?" Anita asked.

"The Interplanet Council's in a special session by video hookup. They've just finished voting. It's a tie!"

Chapter Eleven

"Oh, no!" Tom moaned.

"Uh-huh. That means this year's chairman casts the deciding vote," Gene Larson said.

"And guess who that is," Anita added. "Our friend Marcus Overmann."

"My father seems to think he can bring Overmann around," Tom told the others.

"And what do you think?" Anita asked.

"I don't see how he can!"

Later that day, Tom and his friends were gathered in Larson's office to watch the final vote of the Interplanet Council. Mr. Swift was there as well, and Tom caught the slight smile on his lips when the announcer reported that Marcus Overmann had cast the deciding vote for the *Daniel Boone*'s venture into the star worlds.

"Why do I have this funny feeling you knew this was going to happen?" Tom asked. "You don't look all that much surprised."

The elder Swift tried hard to appear bewildered. "Now how can you say that, son? Everyone knows that Marcus Overmann is a reasonable man."

"He is now," Tom said amid the sneers from his friends. "What I want to know is, how did he *get* that way?"

The reporters were interviewing Overmann, and everyone fell silent to listen.

"—and I am proud to have played a small part in furthering the aims of science," Overmann said pompously. "The safety and well-being of these valuable creatures is dear to us all."

"Sir," a reporter asked, "is it true this trip will be named the Overmann Expedition, in your honor?"

"*Whaaaaat!*" Anita Thorwald threw her hands in the air. "You have *got* to be kidding!"

"Hold it down!" snapped Ben.

"It is true I have been so honored." Overmann sighed. "Though undeservedly so. And of course, I will be joining my longtime friend and competitor, Mister Tom Swift Senior, on this upcoming venture."

Gene Larson snapped a pencil in two and looked at the ceiling. "Now just who's idea was that?" He snorted in disgust. "Tell me it wasn't yours, Mister Swift."

"I assure you it wasn't," Tom's father protested. "That was Henry Greylock's contribution, and not a bad one at that, whether we like it or not. All *I* did was show Marcus some figures on the star world trade, *and* what he might lose if he kept bad-mouthing Aquilla and everyone else in interstellar space." He laid a hand on Larson's shoulder. "Look at it this way, Gene—it's going to be nice and quiet here on the Moon for a while."

"Why, you're right." Larson's somber face brightened. "I hadn't thought about that . . ."

The *Daniel Boone* had been outfitted with the stardrive, the fastest method of travel known to man, and the Interplanet Navy had delegated one of their best officers to pilot the ship. Everyone met Captain Susan Travis at dinner the first night aboard, on the eve of the ship's departure. The excitement of the trip had touched crew and passengers alike, and even Marcus Overmann was on his best behavior.

"A momentous occasion!" he boomed heartily. "I'm sure this venture will long be remembered as one of the most vital contributions to our age."

"You're right, Marcus," Mr. Swift agreed, doing his best to keep a straight face.

"Captain," Overmann went on, "tell me about the stardrive that takes us into hyperspace. I've never had the experience—"

"You're sitting right next to its inventor." Susan Travis pointed to Tom. "He can probably tell you better than anyone. Hyperspace, or null space, after all, is a tricky place to be."

"Tricky?" Overmann repeated.

Tom smiled. "Yes, you see, the stardrive creates a magnetic field and dilates space by means of something like an electronic crowbar. Once you're in hyperspace, everything is turned inside out. What would normally take a long time, only takes seconds. Only trouble is, it doesn't feel very pleasant."

"What do you mean?"

"Well," Ben took up the story, "there's that tremendous pressure, and you get nauseous, and then, if it takes too long, you black out."

"Now wait a minute!" Overmann protested, glaring at Tom's father. "No one warned me about this. I—"

"Don't worry about it, Marcus," Mr. Swift said soothingly. "It only takes seconds. People go in and out of hyperspace all the time now."

Overmann opened his mouth, then thought

better of it and unhappily dug into his salad.

Tom liked Captain Susan Travis. She was an attractive, intelligent brunette in her early thirties, a woman who had risen swiftly in the I.P. Navy. On the surface, she was friendly and easy-going. Tom sensed, however, that underneath that calm exterior was a woman to be reckoned with.

Over dessert, Earth's councilor Henry Greylock complimented her on the way the *Daniel Boone* had taken shape under her command.

"A really marvelous ship," he said. "One of the finest I've ever seen."

"I can't take much credit for that," the captain told him. "Mister Swift is responsible for the *Daniel Boone*'s performance."

"Oh, I certainly give credit where credit is due, Swift," Overmann said offhandedly. "But as I always say, a ship's only as good as its captain. Perhaps, when we get under way, Captain Travis, you could take a little time to show me around."

"I'd be glad to," she replied. "Though I expect there's very little you haven't already seen."

"Eh?" Overmann's hawklike face raised up from his plate. "Why, I haven't seen *anything* yet."

"You didn't go on the tour?"

"The regular tour?" Overmann shrugged. "No, I didn't bother with that."

"I'm sorry you didn't," Captain Travis said. "It's the only one we have, Councilor."

Overmann chuckled. "But I want to see the nuclear fusion engines, the stardrive—that sort of thing."

"I'm afraid that's impossible. Those areas are strictly off limits."

"Off limits!" Overmann looked as if he might choke on his ice cream. "May I remind you that I'm an I.P. councilor, Captain!"

"You may."

"Now, look here—"

"There's a reason for tight security," she explained, "particularly on this trip. It's no reflection on you, sir."

"Well, that's just fine." Overmann dismissed her without a glance.

"No, it is not just fine," Susan Travis said pointedly. The Lunar councilor looked up, startled at this woman he'd taken so lightly. "I may be telling you something you already know," she went on, "but I think you'd better listen. I'm not just talking about routine ship's security. There's more to it than that."

Overmann laid down his fork. "We *all* know what's been happening. One of our priceless ecosystems has disappeared." He cast a cutting glance at Tom's father. "That's why the fighters are thick as flies around the *Boone*."

"Yes, sir," Captain Travis said patiently. "But once we start into hyperspace, all the fighters in the world can't help us."

Overmann looked blank.

"You see, before we go into hyperspace, the other craft have to fall back. Otherwise either we'd all blow up, or the warp in the magnetic field would throw us off course and we wouldn't know where we'd end up. So there will be a time when we'll be alone in space. Now, if you were these—mysterious intruders, when would you attack the *Daniel Boone*?"

Overmann stared, his jaw hanging open. "I— didn't realize it was that serious—"

"I'm glad we got it cleared up," the captain said shortly. "If you have any more questions about security, sir, be sure and let me know, will you?"

The curve of the Moon filled half the broad window on the bridge of the *Daniel Boone*, flooding the room with a ghostly yellow light as the ship drifted slowly off to port. Soon the blue crescent of the Earth appeared against a bright band of the Milky Way.

Tom stood with Anita and his father near the

rear of the darkened bridge. He could see Captain Travis and her deck officers bent intently over their winking consoles. In a small area just below Tom's perch, Ben was assisting Lieutenant Phil Markham, the *Boone*'s computer officer.

"We should be gaining speed now," said the elder Swift, glancing at his watch. "Ah—there's our escort."

Tom looked at the big scope projection on the forward bulkhead. To port and starboard of the *Daniel Boone* was a sprinkling of rapidly moving vees, the fast fighter craft of the Lunar States.

"There," Anita said excitedly, "here come the marines!" From a far quadrant to port appeared a thick cluster of blips joining the L.S. forces— heavily armed *Lancer* class ships of the U.S. Space Navy.

"Can't say I'm not glad to see them," said Tom's father. "I don't think our mysterious foes will be too anxious to show their faces. At least not while those fellows are around!"

Hours later, they were in the right position to enter hyperspace.

"Six minutes and counting," droned a toneless voice over the speaker. "Entry-H Alert."

"Four minutes to shutdown . . ."

"There go our escorts," said Tom. "We're leaving everyone behind."

"Let's hope both our friends *and* our enemies," Anita said under her breath.

"There's nothing on the long-range scope," Tom's father reported. "At this speed, our adversaries would have to be in something incredibly fast to keep up with us."

Tom's fingers ached. He suddenly realized he was nervously squeezing the arms of his padded contour seat. He glanced quickly at Anita, who was strapped in next to him. The redhead stared blankly into the darkened room.

"Eighty seconds . . ."

"Looks like we're going to make it," Tom said tightly. "Another minute and it'll be over."

"Can't happen too soon for me," whispered Anita.

"Seventy-seven . . . seventy-six . . ."

A shrill alarm ripped through the silence of the bridge.

"Blips—five of them and coming in fast!"

Tom stared. There was no need to look at the screen—the black ships were clearly visible through the big port straight ahead.

"They're not after us," Anita cried out. "Look —they're going for the globes!"

Chapter Twelve

Anita was right. The black ships made straight for the shimmering globes circling the *Boone*. The captain shouted orders, sending her officers scurrying over the deck. As she'd feared, the enemy had struck them when the starship was helpless to fight back.

"*Seventy-three . . . seventy-two . . .*" the monotonous voice droned through the speaker.

The dark vessels swarmed about the *Boone*'s precious cargo. Tom knew what the marauders planned, and the thought raised the hairs on the back of his neck. If they couldn't loosen the globes from the starship's grasp, they would destroy them!

"Do you think those ships are manned?" Ben asked.

"If they were, it'd be suicide for the pilots," Tom grumbled. "No, I believe they're dummies guided by remote control. All they have to do is sever the globes from the *Daniel Boone* or destroy them, and if we all get drawn into hyperspace in the process—"

"We'll come out the other side as a brand-new cloud of interstellar garbage!" Anita finished.

"Sixty seconds . . . fifty-nine . . . fifty-eight . . ."

Tom heard Captain Travis give terse orders to the crew, when suddenly one of the spiny vessels veered off its path, nearly colliding with another. The second ship swerved and wobbled off to port.

"What's the matter with them?" said Anita, astonished at these bizarre maneuvers. "Look at that!" Two more of the dark craft nearly hit head on. One spiraled out of the way and fled under the *Daniel Boone*'s hull.

"Forty-two . . . forty-one . . . forty . . ."

"Something's wrong with their guidance systems," Tom said sharply. "See? That's exactly what happens when on-board computers go haywire."

Anita shook her head. "But *all* the computers? That doesn't make sense."

Tom shrugged, then looked again at the attacking vessels. Two had already vanished. They were fading blips, far behind the swiftly moving starship.

"Twenty-one . . . twenty . . . nineteen . . ."

The last two spiny ships abruptly broke off their attack and shot straight up in a wrenching eighty-degree climb. A cheer went up from the bridge.

"Approaching Entry-H, Captain," the computer announced.

"Stand by for transition." Susan Travis's voice was perfectly calm, as if nothing unusual had taken place.

"Three . . . two . . . one . . . ZERO!"

Tom felt the familiar pressure that seemed to crush his body and press the air out of his lungs. His head pounded, and he saw stars in front of his eyes. His stomach turned and—

Suddenly, it was over.

Everything became normal again, and Tom breathed a sigh of relief. A few minutes later, Susan Travis made her way to the computer console and dragged Ben Walking Eagle to his feet. Tom's father looked over his shoulder and waved Tom and Anita over.

"Ben here's our hero of the day." The elder Swift beamed. He pumped Ben's hand, then stood back to let the officers have their turn.

"What on Earth did you do?" asked Anita.

"Not a lot, really," said Ben, color rising to his face.

"You did, too!" Susan Travis said firmly. "Ben's quick thinking got us out of a very bad jam back there. I'm *not* too sure where we'd be right now, but I have a good idea."

"It was the computer, right?" said Tom. "The way those vessels were jerking around all over the sky."

"Right." Ben grinned. "I was on the board during the switchover, and tangled up their programming. The second those ships appeared, I started getting echoes on my screen from their on-board computers. I twisted the stuff around that came through—"

"—and sent it back to the wrong ships," Anita finished with a laugh. "No wonder they were zigzagging all over the place. Every ship's computer was getting guidance commands from another! Ben, that was absolutely brilliant. You're the greatest!"

The young people were sitting in the small utility room off their quarters that Tom turned into a makeshift lab. During the few hours of spare time he had between coming out of hyperspace and their arrival on Aquilla, he'd made a few adjustments to his holoprojector.

Now he turned to K'orlii. "How long has it been since you left Aquilla?" he asked. "Two years? Three? I bet you're anxious to see the old place again."

"I am indeed," the Aquillan sighed. "It has been three years. I'd have returned much sooner if I hadn't met you and Ben." K'orlii grinned. "And Anita, of course. She's the one who got me involved with *SeaGlobe*."

Mr. Swift walked in and perched on the edge of Tom's workbench. "We're in easy range of Aquilla now," he told them. "K'orlii, I've been in touch with your father, and he and your family send their greetings. They're most anxious to see you. But there are a—couple of things you ought to know before we get there." He paused, and ran a hand over his jaw. "I'm afraid not all the news is good."

"My family—!" K'orlii's golden eyes widened in alarm.

"No, no, nothing like that. You know that your father Shaldar and I have worked closely to bring the interests of Earth and Aquilla together. When I saw him six months ago, approval of a long-term agreement by your Twelve Seas Council was all but accomplished." Mr. Swift stopped, and looked grimly at the wall. "Apparently, we are not as close to success as I imagined."

K'orlii looked bewildered. "But my father would do nothing to slow the agreement, I'm certain!"

"No." The elder Swift shook his head. "It's your uncle, Mordan, who's fouling up the works."

K'orlii sat up straight. "I—can't believe that. Uncle Mordan is a fine man. He and my father are quite close."

"Not any more, they're not. Mordan, along with this—K'artar, who is—"

"*K'artar!*" K'orlii's eyes blazed. "My uncle can't be listening to *him*!"

"Exactly who is he?" Tom asked.

"A governor of one of the Twelve Seas," K'orlii replied. "One of the few Aquillans I know who does not believe in our basic philosophy of peace."

"Evidently, he has Mordan's ear now," the elder Swift said. "Your father tells me he's tied up the whole council."

"This business of blaming Aquillans for the troubles around *New America* and the Moon isn't going to help either," Tom added morosely. "Does Mister Overmann know about this?"

"No, but he will soon enough," his father replied. "There are Interplanet personnel on

Aquilla, including one or two who work for the Luna Corporation. I can't keep Overmann from talking to them by deepspace radio."

K'orlii stood up and let out a sigh. "There are some things I need to think about," he said wearily. "I will be in our room if you need me, Tom."

"K'orlii—"

"Please—Tom, I do not wish to talk about it now!"

Tom let him go. "This is a terrific homecoming for K'orlii," he said dully.

"It could get worse," said the elder Swift.

Tom caught the edge in his father's voice. "What do you mean?"

Mr. Swift shrugged. "I just don't like the way things are going. Our enemies have a big, powerful organization at their disposal. One that extends clear to Aquilla, I'm afraid."

"You mean K'orlii's uncle, Mordan?"

"Mordan, and this fellow K'artar. It's quite a coincidence, don't you think? All of a sudden there's trouble on the Twelve Seas Council when there wasn't any before?"

Tom didn't answer. He knew his father was right. The string of near disasters that led from Triton dome, *New America*, and the Moon had followed them through interstellar space to Aquilla. They had not left their mysterious enemy behind. It was already here, waiting for them.

Tom talked to Ben and Anita late in the afternoon, and told them about the conversation with his father. Ben reported that Councilor Overmann had spoken to his friends on Aquilla, and knew all about the trouble there.

"You can bet he gave *them* an earful, too," the boy added. "Made sure he spread all the bad news from the inner planets."

"I cannot stand that man!" blurted Anita. "The Overmann Expedition indeed. Do you honestly think he believes everyone's honoring him for being such a warm and wonderful person? A friend of the endangered species?" She made a face. "It's not right, you know? A troublemaker like Overmann gets away with everything, and a nice guy like K'orlii is—*ashamed* to come out of his room!"

"No," Tom agreed. "Doesn't make a whole lot of sense, does it?"

"We shouldn't let him just sit there and mope," said Ben. "He hasn't done a thing, Tom. I'm going to drop by and talk to him. Can't do any harm."

"I don't think K'orlii's too interested in talking, Ben . . ."

"You never know till you try," Ben said stubbornly, and stomped down the corridor. Tom and Anita, meanwhile, went toward the bridge. Suddenly, they heard a hoarse shout behind them. They turned and saw Ben running toward them, his face pale as chalk.

"K'orlii," Ben burst out, "is not in his cabin, but he's been there—and so has someone else!"

Tom's stomach knotted up at the sight of the room he shared with the young Aquillan. A chair lay broken against the wall. Bedding was ripped apart and scattered everywhere. Clothes, books, and personal belongings were tossed about the room.

"Get the captain and call security," Tom snapped. "I'm going to track him down with Aristotle." Ben and Anita nodded and sprinted off. Tom barged into his makeshift lab where he had left the robot. "Someone's got K'orlii," he explained quickly. "Let's find him—and fast!"

Aristotle's sensing devices hadn't been designed specifically for tracking people, but they served that purpose well. The robot's "sight" ranged from the infrared to the ultraviolet, and his hearing was equally acute. He began tracking K'orlii in a number of different ways: there was an invisible trail where the Aquillan's boots had left small particles behind . . . faint traces of his body heat still lingered in the air . . . there were molecules of moisture floating about that contained chemical chains the robot knew belonged only to K'orlii.

Aristotle led Tom a few yards along the narrow corridor that split the starship, then veered sharply to port and clattered down the stairwell to the lower depths of the hull. The deck thundered under Tom's boots now, for they were directly over the chamber that housed the enormous fusion engines.

"Are you sure he came this way, Aristotle?" Tom asked. "Toward the power well?"

"I am certain," the robot answered. "And I must warn you to be on the alert, Tom, for there is another person with him."

Tom went stiff. "Someone did kidnap him, then!"

"That is highly probable." Aristotle lurched to a stop and jerked up a hand. "Tom—they are very near. I can sense them! Be careful!"

Tom didn't answer. He was already down the hall, far ahead of the robot. Turning a corner, he almost tripped over the body of a young security guard, who was sprawled on the deck before the open lock to the power room. An ugly trickle of blood coursed down his cheek and stained the silver collar of his jumpsuit.

Chapter Thirteen

Aristotle bent down, letting the senses in his fingers brush lightly over the man's face and arms. "He is all right. Only minor medical help will be required."

"Good," Tom said with relief. "Help should be close behind." He came to his feet and started for the open lock.

"I advise you to wait," Aristotle warned. "It would be most dangerous to proceed."

"It'll be dangerous for K'orlii if we don't," Tom said impatiently, stepping through the door. Power shook the floor in the room inside. The big nuclear engines hunched in the eerie light like giant, sleeping animals. Tom moved cautiously around the shadowed walls, following the robot's senses. Aristotle paused and pointed upwards. "There, Tom. K'orlii and one other went that way."

Tom's eyes followed the narrow ladder into the gloom. "What's up there—can you tell?"

"A catwalk circles this room. My ultraviolet and infrared scans show no visible persons, but their body heat is quite evident."

"Are there any other doors?"

"Two. One emergency lock on this level, and another up there. They are controlled by the bridge alarm and cannot be opened from in here."

"Fine," Tom said grimly, starting up the ladder. "We're all in here together, then."

"Once more, I must caution against this—"

Tom crept along the high catwalk, thankful that Aristotle's senses could penetrate the darkness. It gave him a small edge, at least—an advantage he'd likely need.

"Wait." The robot stopped him with an open steel palm. "Up there, Tom."

"How far?"

"Twenty-two yards. That thick column of piping. Behind that."

"Does he have a weapon? Can you tell?"

"There is metal on his person. It is not the

proper mass for a weapon. Still—Tom, where are you going?"

"After him," Tom said over his shoulder.

"No, wait for the others," the robot warned. "That metal he carries—"

Tom was already gone. He sprinted for the piping, keeping as low as he could, then pressed himself to the wall and listened. All he could hear was the throb of the giant engines. In a moment, he edged gingerly around the corner.

A dark shape swooped down on his back, slamming him to the floor. Tom realized, too late, that his attacker had climbed above him. The man had hung there in the maze of pipes and waited.

Tom struggled against the assailant's fierce grip, reached for a muscular arm, and felt it twist out of his grasp. He lashed out with his fists and grabbed a tangle of cloth. But the intruder slipped out of his black cloak and ran off. Grinding his teeth in anger, Tom threw away the heavy cloak and ran after the fleeing figure.

"Stop!" he yelled. "There's no place to run!"

The man was fast, but Tom quickly cut the distance between them. Just another few yards and he'd have him. Abruptly, the man turned and leaped to the railing in a crouch. In one motion his hand dipped quickly under his arm, then jerked out at Tom.

Glittering fragments of light came straight for the young inventor's head. He leaped aside, but realized it was a useless maneuver.

Suddenly, the robot's hands slammed hard against his back. Tom sprawled to the floor and rolled. Tiny bits of metal whined past his ears and rattled off Aristotle's chest. Tom came to his feet in time to see the mechanoid's hands flail out in a blur, swatting the last of the deadly missiles aside.

"Mechanical hornets," Aristotle said. "One sting from those, Tom—"

"Never mind that. Where is he?" Before the robot could answer, Tom heard a low moan to his left, saw movement there, and ran toward it.

"K'orlii! Are you all right?" Tom looked over his shoulder. "Aristotle—get us some help up here."

"Help has already arrived," Aristotle reported. "They are in the power room below."

Tom turned back to K'orlii. "Hey, friend—you're going to be fine. Can you tell me what happened?"

"I—don't think so," K'orlii said shakily. He sat up and shook his head. "Where am I?"

"On a catwalk above the fusion engines."

K'orlii looked bewildered. "Fusion engines? "All I remember is, I was in our room and—that's it. Nothing!"

"A drug was applied to your face in liquid form," Aristotle put in. "Probably with a cloth. Residue is still in the air. I would identify it as Chlorafexxo-Nine."

"I didn't smell a thing." K'orlii blinked. "Or see anyone, either."

Captain Travis ran up with four security guards. She glanced at K'orlii, then sent the guards scrambling off in a search. "Are you all right?" she said anxiously. "We'll get some med-techs up here immediately."

"I think he's okay," Tom told her. "Captain, I tangled with the guy, right here. Not three minutes ago. He has to be *some*where."

"I don't suppose you got a good look at him?"

Tom shrugged. "A cloak and a mask. That's about it." He told her about the robot hornets, then helped K'orlii to his feet. The Aquillan was still shaky, and was eased down the ladder to the floor of the power chamber by Tom and Aristotle. Outside in the hall, a guard snapped a salute at Susan Travis.

"Mason's going to be all right, Captain," he reported. "A slight concussion, maybe, but that's all."

"I don't suppose he saw anything, either," Susan Travis said tightly.

"No, Captain. Nothing at all."

"That figures, doesn't it? And no one's in the power room, or anywhere else. Must have had access to the emergency lock. Even though I don't see how!"

"If there was anyone in that room—which I very much doubt!"

"Wh-what?" Tom looked over his shoulder at the gaunt figure of Marcus Overmann, and stood up, trying hard to hold back his anger. "Just what is it you're trying to say, Councilor?"

"Tom's right," Captain Travis added. "I think you'd better explain yourself."

"It's not me that has explaining to do." Overmann's eyes flashed at K'orlii. "It's that person, Captain. The Aquillan spy aboard this vessel."

"That is a—lie!" K'orlii exploded.

"Oh?" Overmann's smile was cold as ice. "And I suppose this is a lie, too." He opened his hand and thrust it under Susan Travis's nose. A small crystal message cube rested in his palm.

"What is this?"

"Henry—" Overmann called over his shoulder. "Tell them what happened, will you? I do not want the captain to have to take *my* word for this."

Henry Greylock walked up to the group, deliberately avoiding K'orlii's glance. "We—ah— spotted this down the hall," he said gruffly.

"Marcus and I were right behind you and the guards. I think you'd better listen to it."

"I will," Susan Travis told him, "as soon as I get to my quarters."

"I'd—rather you heard it right now," Overmann insisted.

Susan Travis jerked the small cube out of his hand and clicked it into the player on her belt. The unit hissed a moment, then a tinny voice spoke in an urgent whisper:

> . . . I hope you're getting this, K'orlii . . . you should be in range of Aquilla now, and I'll try to make it quick. Keep close to Tom Swift and the others, and learn everything you can. . . . Things are coming to a head here. The agreement will not be approved by the Twelve Seas Council. I promise you that!

The unit hissed again with interstellar static, then fell into silence.

"Well?" Overmann beamed triumphantly. "What more do you need? That voice is Shaldar's, the boy's father."

"Our *supposed* friend on Aquilla," Greylock added.

"That thing is a fake and you know it!" K'orlii shouted. He strained to get at Overmann, but Tom held him back.

"It's you who are the fake here," Overmann said sharply, pointing an accusing finger at the Aquillan. "You *met* this so-called hooded intruder, young man, but he didn't carry you off at all. When Tom Swift found you, you had to pretend to be a victim. You tried the same nonsense on *New America*, and then on the Moon. I think it is high time we put an end to this masquerade." Overmann's eyes touched Susan Travis. "Lock him up, Captain. Now!"

"Is that an order, Councilor?" Susan Travis asked coolly.

"Captain," Marcus Overmann spluttered, "is there any *doubt* in your mind about what is going *on* here? You heard the evidence with your own ears!"

"That message cube is no evidence at all," Tom put in. "It's not hard to fake something like this."

"*This* message is quite real," Overmann said stiffly.

Tom glanced at Captain Travis. "Would you excuse me for a moment?" Without waiting for an answer, he pulled Aristotle aside and spoke to him. A few seconds later, a small utility drawer in the robot's chest snapped open. Tom withdrew an object and walked back to the group.

"Now—would you mind playing this, captain?"

"What's going on here," Overmann asked suspiciously.

"Just listen, sir."

Susan Travis clicked the cube into her player:

> *. . . Somebody listen to me, please. I have evidence that Captain Susan Travis and the ship's cook are enemy agents. They're planning to blow up Earth and the Moon tonight!*

"Wh-why, that's *my* voice!" Marcus Overmann stared at the captain, appalled. "I never said anything like that!"

"No," Tom explained, "Aristotle did. He took your voice pattern and recorded the message I gave him. It's the simplest thing in the world. Anyone with an ordinary voice analyzer can do it."

Overmann's face went red. "That has— nothing to do with this!" he raged. "Captain, you are deliberately trying to protect this spy."

"Right," said Susan Travis, a slight smile on her lips. "I am also trying to protect myself, of course. After all, you *did* accuse me and the cook of plotting to disintegrate the inner planets. . . ."

Less than three hours after Tom's encounter with the hooded intruder, the *Daniel Boone* hurtled toward the sea world of Aquilla. It was one of the most beautiful sights Tom had ever seen. Nearly eighty percent of its surface was covered with water, which made the planet shine like a blue-green jewel. Captain Travis brought the starship into a matching orbit two hundred miles above the coral island chain of Kh'lai. Aristotle was delegated to help the crew tend to the *Daniel Boone*, while Tom, his father, and his friends went to the surface in the first shuttle. Marcus Overmann was furious at being left behind. He insisted he had every right to be first on the ground.

"Marcus," Tom's father said firmly, "if I could keep you up here in the *Boone* the whole trip, I'd do it. What I *can* do is make certain you don't start a small war the minute we step ashore."

Overmann ranted and raved, but Mr. Swift simply walked off and left him fuming.

"There!" K'orlii pointed excitedly out the narrow port of the shuttle. "That's Kh'lai, the four-hundred-mile island chain that curls around Aquilla like a hook. That's what Kh'lai means, as a matter of fact. The hook."

"It's gorgeous!" Anita exclaimed. "And where's your island, Rha'mae?"

"Right there. At the bend of the hook."

The shuttle circled once, cut its atmospheric jets, and glided to a smooth landing in the bay off Than'oorii, Rah'mae's major city. Anita gazed in wonder at the delicate, coral spires of the Aquillan buildings, clustered in greenery past a dazzling white beach.

"That's nothing," K'orlii told her. "You ought to see the rest of the city."

"What?" Anita looked puzzled.

"Only about a fifth shows above the water," K'orlii explained. "Probably less than that. The rest is below the surface. Remember, we're amphibious. There's some null-gravity architecture down there you wouldn't believe."

"Now *that* I've got to see," Ben said.

"Architecture and genetic engineering don't have much to do with each other on Earth," said K'orlii. "But here they work together closely. We've *taught* our coral life to build the kind of cities we want. It doesn't harm the ecology of the reef system, and it makes for some fantastic design."

Tom had seen plenty of Aquillans before, but never so many in one place. They crowded onto the narrow causeway to greet K'orlii, and stared with friendly curiosity at the people from Earth. Communication would be easy thanks to the teacher-translator unit Tom had developed. Each of the visitors carried one at all times.

Turning his unit on, the elder Swift walked up to Shaldar, K'orlii's father, and motioned for Tom to follow.

"Old friend, I greet you again with great pleasure," the Aquillan said warmly. "And you as well, young Tom Swift."

Tom shook hands with Shaldar and introduced Ben Walking Eagle and Anita Thorwald. The Aquillans were enthralled with Anita's red hair. In spite of their formal manner, they stared openly at the bright, flaming tresses.

"I apologize for us all," Shaldar said gravely. "I hope you are not offended, Anita."

"She's not." K'orlii laughed. "Father, the only way you can offend a girl from Earth is to *not* show her any attention."

"K'orlii!" Anita tried hard to look shocked.

K'orlii's father sensed that the young people were joking and no one had been offended. He led his party up the beach.

"Everybody walks on Aquilla," K'orlii explained, "unless we go island hopping and the distance is pretty far. Then we ride Salamanda-ris. They're amphibious too, you know."

"What's a Salamandari?" Ben asked.

"One of those." K'orlii pointed to an Aquillan mounted on a long, sleek-skinned creature with razor-honed teeth. It had a bright yellow under-side and a back covered in pale splotches of olive. Its legs looked strong and powerful, with web-bing between the clawed toes. The thing looked to Ben like an eel that had decided to be a lizard or a frog at the last minute.

"Will we be—ah—traveling for any long dis-tances?" he asked warily.

K'orlii laughed. "Don't worry. They're not nearly as nasty as they look."

"Don't see how they could be," Ben muttered. "Anyway, I like to walk, K'orlii. As a matter of fact—"

Ben stopped as thunder rolled across the clear skies overhead, and the second shuttle from the *Daniel Boone* arced in over the atoll and splashed down to a landing.

"Oh, here comes Overmann." Anita groaned. "I knew we were having too much fun."

Chapter Fourteen

Tom's father came back from a long meeting with the Twelve Seas Council, looking grim and tired. "I'm afraid things are worse than we thought," he reported. "Mordan's a decent enough person, but this K'artar has filled his head with a great deal of misinformation about Earth and the Inner Planets." Mr. Swift sank down in a chair and squinted at the bright blue sea. "Neither Mordan nor K'artar have ever been off-planet, Tom. As far as I've been able to learn, anyway."

"Which means someone else is feeding that stuff to them," Tom finished.

"Exactly. K'artar's in someone's pay."

"You know, right from the start, I've figured Marcus Overmann had a hand in this," Tom pointed out.

"He very well may have. I wouldn't put it past him." Mr. Swift frowned and studied his hands. "The only thing is, if he is mixed up with K'artar, they're putting on a great act for the Twelve Seas Council. A couple of times today I thought Marcus and K'artar were going to break up the meeting and start slugging it out right there. If Henry Greylock hadn't smoothed things over, I think we'd all be back on the *Boone* now, headed straight for Earth."

Tom thought about that. "I guess they would act that way, if they were really up to something."

"Of course," his father agreed. "That's exactly what they'd do." He stopped, and stared up at the coral ceiling. "I'm afraid you'll get a chance to see their performance for yourself, Tom. Shaldar's invited Mordan and K'artar to dinner. Along with our crowd from the starship. Just a small family get-together."

Tom moaned. "I can hardly wait!"

For a while, he thought his father's worst fears might prove unfounded. Shaldar had tactfully seated Mordan and K'artar at the far end of the long table, away from Marcus Overmann and the rest of the party from Earth. Overmann was making a real effort to be amiable and charming, and Henry Greylock was right beside him, to make sure it stayed that way.

Seated next to K'orlii's mother, Therlaia, was a slim, pretty Aquillan girl who couldn't keep her eyes off K'orlii. Tom finally pried her name out of his friend.

"That's B'teia," the Aquillan said casually. "Just an old friend from my school days."

"A good-looking old friend, too," Ben said.

K'orlii turned a darker shade of blue. "That's exactly what she is," he stammered, "a—a friend!"

"Sure," Ben said idly, "that's what I said, isn't it?" Tom cleared his throat, and Anita hid a grin behind her napkin.

"You might like to know," Therlaia told Tom, "that this table we are eating on is probably the largest piece of wood on Aquilla. It's spiderlime, from the planet Arborea. A gift from your father."

Tom admired the delicate yellow grain. He knew it was one of the best of the many fine woods that came from that forested world. "I guess there isn't much wood on Aquilla, is there?" he said.

"Just the little you've seen," Therlaia replied. "And a few trees that grow on our islands. Very much like your palms, I believe. Of course, they're so rare no one would dream of cutting one down."

"Not like they do on Earth!" K'artar grinned at the end of the table. "Wasting their resources."

Shaldar looked embarrassed. Marcus Overmann opened his mouth, but Tom's father beat him to it. "You are quite right," he said politely. "We *did* make that mistake. We've taken a great many steps to correct it. *Ark Two* is a part of those measures."

K'artar was heavier than most Aquillan men, who tended to be slim-waisted, with the broad shoulders of swimmers. His golden eyes roamed the table a moment, then rested on Henry Greylock. "The I.P. councilor from Earth explained your problems very well at our meeting this afternoon. Don't you think so, Mordan?"

K'orlii's uncle nodded but said nothing.

"That is one of our reasons for being here," Greylock said amiably. "If there's anything you don't understand about our program—"

"Oh, I *understand* it very well indeed," K'artar interrupted. "The people of Earth have ravaged their own planet, and now they want to destroy the star worlds!"

"Mister K'artar—please!" Greylock's mustache twisted nervously.

"I will not sit here and—*listen* to this!" Marcus

Overmann burst out. He jerked to his feet and shook a fist at K'artar. "You and I are in agreement on one thing, sir. *As long as I have a vote, there will never be a pact between Aquilla and the inner planets. Never!*" With that, he turned and stormed out of the room.

K'orlii's father looked stunned while K'artar and Mordan watched the Lunar councilor leave, satsified grins stretching their blue-shaded faces.

Aquilla's sun warmed the vast expanse of water and turned the beaches a dazzling white. Ben, Tom, and Anita waited on the shore, making final adjustments to their drysuits. The outing they'd planned the day before had turned into a less than happy occasion. Tom's father and Shaldar were doing their best to get the Aquillans and I.P. representatives back together. So far, however, Overmann and K'artar had refused to step into the same room.

"It looks to me like every world has at least *one* Marcus Overmann," Anita said testily. "We've got ours, and Aquilla's got K'artar."

"They're a great pair," Tom agreed. "Oh, look, there's K'orlii and B'teia!"

The two Aquillans emerged from the depths off the reef and came ashore. K'orlii grinned at his friends.

"All ready to see the other half of our planet?"

He turned to the blue-skinned girl. "Bring them up, B'teia."

"Bring what—" Ben started to say, then stared in disbelief.

K'orlii laughed. "Come on, this is the chance of a lifetime. You're one of the few off-planet visitors who's ever had the privilege of riding a Salamandari."

"That's what it is, huh? A privilege? I'm sure glad you told me," Ben grumbled. He cast a suspicious eye at the five creatures B'teia led into the shallows. He hadn't cared for the serpentlike animals the day before, and didn't like them any better now. One curled a long, yellow-green neck in his direction and opened its jaws to show a mouthful of teeth.

Ben shook his head. "Uh-uh. Thanks, but no thanks."

"I thought the Cherokees were able to ride anything," quipped Anita.

"Anything reasonable," Ben corrected. "*That* is not a reasonable beast, Anita."

"Oh, it is very tame," B'teia spoke up. "Here. You must give it a try." She looked at Ben with immense golden eyes. "Please? I would be honored if you took my favorite, Phardaar." She laid a hand on the creature to her left—the one that had just bared its teeth.

"That's Phardaar, is it?" Ben glanced at Tom. "I should've guessed, right?"

In spite of Ben's concern, the Salamandaris proved to be docile, reliable underwater mounts. K'orlii and B'teia led their dry-suited guests out of the shallows into deeper water below, then circled back to the undersea portion of the city of Than'oorii.

"There it is." K'orlii pointed. "Straight ahead!"

At first, none of the visitors could see anything resembling a city. High, graceful peaks of white and pink coral stretched up from the depths, their tips forming the chain reef of Kh'lai. Multi-colored fish darted in and out of the lacy structure.

Suddenly, Tom realized that not all the creatures swimming through the coral caverns were fish. A great many of them were Aquillans! Abruptly, the tall structures before his eyes took on an entirely different meaning.

"We *are* amphibians, you know," said K'orlii, guiding them swiftly around the spires of the city. "People tend to forget that, even good friends like you, who know us well. Than'oorii and our other cities are built to let us live in the sea as much as we like. Of course, there are air chambers everywhere, and we keep them continually oxygenated."

"Then, you *could* actually live underwater all the time, couldn't you?" asked Ben.

"Most of the time, certainly," B'teia said. "But I don't think any Aquillan would care for that. We love the sun too much."

The Salamandaris sped them quickly away from the city, high above the crystal ocean floor. Occasionally, great schools of fish appeared in the distance, so dense they shut out the light from the sun. B'teia explained that these were controlled, migratory fish farms, part of the planet's major crop.

The two Aquillans led their friends in a sharp course past a small mountain of yellow coral. On the other side of this formation, the sea bottom disappeared abruptly and fell away into a dark, blue-black abyss. K'orlii pulled his mount to a halt and signaled the others to stop.

"Good grief," gasped Anita, "I'm not sure I believe that!"

"It's an offshoot of the Dharmaii Trench," K'orlii explained. "Only about sixty-two thousand feet here. It gets deeper further out."

"Deeper?" Tom shook his head. "The Mindanao Deep off the Philippines is around thirty-five thousand. You could drop nearly two of them in that thing."

"Does anything—live down there?" Anita asked.

"Oh, yes. Some fascinating creatures," B'teia replied. "Most of them are quite harmless. And of course, some dangerous fish that couldn't survive up here."

"It is the—ah—specimens that live around the shallower parts of the Dharmaii you have to look out for," K'orlii said casually, nodding his head off to port.

Tom looked, and for a moment saw nothing. Then, the sand whipped away in a storm and something flat, gray, and enormous streaked through a cloud of silt for the deeps.

Tom gasped. "Whatever that was, it wasn't much smaller than a football field."

The Aquillan nodded. "You are right. It was a good-sized young Throo'n, about eighty, maybe eighty-five yards wide. When it grows up—"

"When it what?" asked Ben.

"Why, yes. They get a lot bigger than that."

"Why don't we sort of wander on back?" Tom suggested. "Before its daddy gets home from work?"

K'orlii grinned. "They don't generally harm anyone, but we shouldn't linger around the trench, at any rate. There are a lot of other creatures more aggressive than the Throo'n."

It didn't seem to Tom like the time or the place to ask just what those creatures might be.

The Aquillans guided them west, then south

again past the reef that housed the city of Than'oorii. Far across the sea flats they glimpsed the shadow of another great reef, which K'orlii explained was Lha'ii, a very small islet in the long Kh'lai chain.

"It contains a research station and a very small population. The beach is spectacular, though. If your people are here long enough—" K'orlii stopped himself and gritted his teeth. "We keep coming back to that, don't we?"

"Maybe we could take Overmann and K'artar on an outing," Tom mused. "On the way, we could drop by and show them that baby Throo'n."

K'orlii grinned. "Don't tempt me, please. We Aquillans are supposed to be peace-loving people. Remember?"

"It isn't always easy to keep that in mind," B'teia said sadly, her long, ebony hair floating like dark grass about her head. "K'artar I understand. But K'orlii's uncle Mordan—he has always been such a likeable man."

"Hold it," Tom said suddenly, wheeling his mount next to K'orlii's. "What's—that? Anything you recognize? A research station or something?"

K'orlii peered in the direction of Tom's arm. There was a dim white glow, far to the east, partially obscured by a high coral reef. "I haven't the slightest idea," he said finally. "Whatever it is, it doesn't belong there." Pressing his legs firmly against the Salamandari, he urged the creature forward. Tom and the others followed.

"We can see it better from up there," said K'orlii, moving swiftly over a bed of red sponges. "There's a cool current near the bottom that—" He stopped and went rigid. A small cry of anguish stuck in his throat. "Tom—it can't be! Not here on Aquilla!"

"It is," Tom said flatly.

From the bed of red sponges, the ocean floor dropped sharply away into another broad arm of the Dharmaii Trench. Nearly lost in the shadows of that great depression was the unmistakable silvery curve of *SeaGlobe*.

Chapter Fifteen

"Tom, what's *SeaGlobe* doing on Aquilla?" Anita asked, shaking her head in disbelief.

"It's K'artar's work!" K'orlii said bitterly. "It has to be. I hate to admit that Marcus Overmann's right. There *are* traitors on Aquilla. We're in this up to our necks!"

"But he didn't do it alone," Tom said. "Someone else is involved. He gazed through the water. "I want a closer look at that globe. Maybe we can learn something."

"Tom," Anita said, "that is *not* a good idea!"

"It's a terrible idea," K'orlii agreed. "But he's right. They can't have just left *SeaGlobe* there in the trench. There have to be support systems, personnel, to keep things going. Could be our only chance to learn who else is behind this." K'orlii paused. "I'm going with you, Tom. The rest of you get back to Than'oorii."

"No way!" Ben protested.

"Someone has to get help!" K'orlii insisted. "It won't do any good if we all get in trouble down there. B'teia—get some sea patrol riders and send them as quickly as you can. Make certain they do *not* wear the house sign of either K'artar or Mordan. I have no idea who we can trust anymore. Even in our own city."

"Be very careful, K'orlii," warned the Aquillan girl. "You, too, Tom Swift."

Tom nodded.

K'orlii knew the currents well, and moved quickly down to the lower depths, keeping a high ridge of coral between him and the distance *SeaGlobe*. Tom followed close behind.

When the Aquillan finally stopped under a clump of wavering sea plants, the young inventor glanced at his watch and noticed a good twenty minutes had passed.

"It doesn't look as if we're much closer than we were," he said thoughtfully.

"We are, though." K'orlii explained. "You've forgotten just how big *SeaGlobe* is, Tom. And distances are very deceiving under water." He hesitated. "I'll have to go on alone from here."

"What are you talking about!" Tom protested.

"Depth and pressure. Even with your drysuit, you can't get close to the rim of the Dharmaii Trench. Neither can the Salamandaris."

"You didn't mention this before."

"Why should I? It would have changed nothing, would it?" He slipped off his mount and handed the guiding cords to Tom. "Don't look like that. I'll be all right. I was born here, remember?"

"I'm trying to."

"You know what?" said K'orlii. "Right at this moment, so am I."

Tom watched K'orlii's pale blue shadow, almost invisible against the sandy ocean floor. The Aquillan circled over the ridge, then finally disappeared from sight. Tom didn't like the idea of just waiting, but he knew his friend was right. K'orlii was in his own element, while he, in spite of his undersea experience, would always be a stranger in this green-hued world.

Suddenly, he leaned over the Salamandari's neck and squinted in the direction where K'orlii had disappeared. There was something, only— there! There it was again!

Six immense, torpedo-shaped shadows moved swiftly over the sandy floor, sniffing after K'orlii's trail like great, lean hounds. Broad tiger stripes covered their flanks, and Tom knew they were sharks, the biggest he'd ever seen! None of them was shorter than seventy feet!

He urged his mount past the ridge, forcing it over the sands toward K'orlii. The sharks were circling rapidly just overhead. Didn't K'orlii see them? Tom's heart sank. The Aquillan was too intent on his task. At any other time, he would have sensed the danger above him. Now, he was blind to everything but the far dome of *SeaGlobe*.

Tom plunged his Salamandari through a forest of sea fern. Below, he caught a quick glimpse of K'orlii against the sand. One of the striped monsters veered off from the others and nosed down behind the unwary swimmer.

"K'orlii!" Tom shouted into the com on his wrist. "K'orlii, behind you!" But the Aquillan was still too far away for the short-range signal to reach him.

The shark swerved to the right, stirring up a great cloud of silt. When Tom saw it again, it was skimming the sandy floor, hurtling like a missile toward the Aquillan.

Tom wrenched his mount to a stop, jerked out his utility blade, and rapped it hard against his belt. The loud sound of metal on metal rang sharply through the water. K'orlii looked over his shoulder and saw several thousand pounds of bone and teeth streaking toward him. He threw himself aside, rolling head over heels in the water. The shark bolted past him another thirty yards, snapped its great jaws angrily, and turned its enormous bulk in pursuit.

K'orlii dove headlong into a thicket of sea grass. The shark went after him, leaving a heavy cloud of sand and uprooted plants in its wake. Tom forced his frightened Salamandari into the depths.

"K'orlii!" he called sharply, "up here—quick!"

This time the Aquillan heard him clearly. The shark nosed after him. K'orlii let him come at him, then jerked aside and churned the water in Tom's direction. Tom moved straight at his friend. K'orlii reached out, grabbed Tom's shoulder and hung on. The giant shape tore out of the sea fern and plunged after the pair. Tom kicked the Salamandari hard in the ribs. The terrified creature needed no urging—it knew very well what was after it.

"There's no way," K'orlii cried. "You can't outrun one of those things!"

Tom didn't answer. A shadow darkened the sand in his path. Then another and another. A locomotive-sized monster was right on their heels, and the rest of the bunch was moving swiftly down from above.

He risked a look over his shoulder and wished he hadn't. There was nothing to see but a great red cavern, and teeth as long as his arm. Two more sharks streaked by in front, leaving a shock wave of water in their path.

"Tom—hard a'port, fast!" K'orlii shouted.

Tom wrenched the Salamandari to his left. An enormous wall of tiger-striped hide rumbled past in a frothy storm.

"Take him to the bottom," snapped K'orlii. "It's the only chance we've—oh, no!"

Three of the creatures were coming at them from below. The one behind would be turning, driving them right into the others.

Suddenly, the huge sea beasts stopped, turned on their tails, and streaked off in a fast retreat!

Tom stared, unable to believe what he was seeing. "We didn't scare them," he told K'orlii. "What did?"

"There." K'orlii pointed past him to the right.

A dozen sea patrol riders approached on fast, motorized sleds. Each carried a slim sonic rifle, the weapons that had put the giant sharks to flight. Ben, Anita, and B'teia trailed the group on Salamandaris.

The first rider pulled his machine on its tail

and grinned at K'orlii. "Having a little striper trouble, son?"

"Worse than that, Thor'ae," K'orlii replied. "Did B'teia tell you?"

"Something about *SeaGlobe*, the missing ecosystem." Thor'ae looked narrowly at K'orlii. "You didn't really see that thing, did you?"

The young Aquillan sighed. "I don't want it to be there any more than you do, but it is. Come on, I'll show you."

Sea patrol riders circled high above the great crevice, powerful spotlights from their sleds stabbing ribbons into the gloom. After half an hour of searching, Thor'ae brought his machine back to the shallows and called off his men.

"I don't know what you people *thought* you saw," he said soberly, "but there's nothing down there now."

"There's *got* to be!" K'orlii insisted. "We saw it, all of us!"

"I'm sure you saw something," said Thor'ae. "But it certainly wasn't *SeaGlobe*."

"Maybe it's further down," Anita suggested.

Thor'ae shook his head. "We swept the place clean with our instruments. If I were you I would forget the whole thing. There's no great hurry to lay shame at Aquilla's door."

Before K'orlii could answer, Thor'ae gunned

his sled into action and whirred off for his men.

K'orlii sighed. "We saw something, Tom. All of us did. Whether I want to or not, I would be willing to swear it was *SeaGlobe*."

"Oh, we saw it," Tom agreed. "Only we don't have any way to prove it."

Tom and K'orlii had a good idea what would happen when word got out about their so-called "sighting" of the missing *SeaGlobe* in Aquillan waters. On their way to the surface, they decided that they should get the news to Shaldar and the elder Swift as soon as possible. Tom's father could keep Overmann from blowing his stack, and Shaldar would handle K'artar and Mordan. But when they came ashore they realized it was too late for that. The beach was crowded with Aquillans, and none of them looked friendly.

"The patrol called ahead on their radios," K'orlii said. "We forgot about that."

K'artar didn't wait for them to reach dry land. At his signal, armed Aquillans waded into the surf, jerked the riders roughly off their mounts, and pushed them ashore.

K'orlii angrily shook off his guard. His golden eyes flashed at K'artar, then rested on his uncle. "Can't you do your own thinking any more?" he lashed out. "Does K'artar have to do it for you?"

"Now, now—ah—K'orlii." Mordan blinked.

"It's—all for the best, boy. You'll see. These Earth people are nothing but trouble . . ." He looked reassuringly at K'artar. "Yes—nothing but trouble, young man!"

"I demand that you let me go," K'orlii said sharply. "And my friends as well. When my father—"

"Your father?" K'artar's thin lips curled into a grin. "He has nothing to say in Aquillan affairs. Not anymore."

"What—do you mean? He's—"

"He is *nothing*!" K'artar exploded. "Nothing more than a traitor to Aquilla. As you are, and the girl here!" He glanced quickly at B'teia, then back to K'orlii. "You had a choice, both of you. You chose the Earth, and turned your back on your own world."

"What—have you done to my father?" K'orlii demanded. "Where is he?"

"Locked up, where he belongs."

"Locked up? You wouldn't dare do that!"

"We will deal with Shaldar and the rest of you when these Earth people are gone," K'artar snarled.

"Just what is it we're supposed to have done?" Tom asked. "Seems to me you forgot to get around to that."

"Don't take me for a fool, Tom Swift!" the

Aquillan shouted. "Did you think you could get away with that—blaming Aquilla for stealing your bowl full of fish?" K'artar threw back his head and laughed. "We don't *need* any more fish, or anything else from you. We've got plenty of everything right here. We will not have Earth's water in our seas!"

Tom tried to speak, but the Aquillans around K'artar caught the fever of the man's speech and cheered him on. Suddenly, Tom and his friends were engulfed in an angry tide of bodies, and it was all their guards could do to get them safely to their quarters.

"I've already tried to reach the *Boone*, but they won't let me use their equipment." The elder Swift sighed wearily. "And if I did reach our people, then what? Just what K'artar would like —Earth forces *invading* Aquilla. We can't win, son."

"Did the rest of the Twelve Seas Council go along with this?" Tom asked.

"What council?" his father said bluntly. "It's just a name now, and no more. K'artar's fooled them all, at least for the time being. The whole bunch is eating out of his hands. They're convinced we're here to take over."

"What for?"

"Who knows?" Mr. Swift shrugged. "I don't think the council has even bothered to ask. Besides, an unknown danger is far worse than one you can see, right? That's how K'artar got to them. Then, when word came back that you'd supposedly tried to stick them with the theft of *SeaGlobe* . . ." He paused and looked curiously at his son. "What exactly *did* you see down there, Tom?"

Tom sank down wearily and squinted at the brassy afternoon sun. "We all saw *SeaGlobe*. And when the patrol got there—*Poof!* It was gone, vanished."

"It simply doesn't make sense," the elder Swift muttered.

"What's supposed to happen to us now?" Tom asked.

"According to K'artar, we get kicked off Aquilla first thing in the morning. Overmann and Greylock are in their quarters. Marcus has thrown a dozen fits already, of course."

"I'm not too worried about us," Tom said thoughtfully. "I don't think K'artar's crazy enough to harm us with the *Boone* hovering up there. Shaldar though, and the rest of K'orlii's family . . ." Tom let his words trail away.

"You are wrong, Mister Swift—very wrong indeed!"

Tom and his father turned, startled at the soft voice behind them.

"B'teia!" Tom exclaimed. "How did *you* get in here!"

"I slipped away," the Aquillan girl said hastily, "after I overheard some of K'artar's people talking. We Aquillans are not the only ones in danger. He does not plan to let you leave the planet alive!"

Chapter Sixteen

Tom's father slammed a fist into his open palm. "K'artar must be out of his mind to think he could get away with that. He has a handful of Aquillans stirred up with his lies, but that's *not* the whole planet!"

"You are right," sighed B'teia. "But that handful is enough to destroy those of us who stand against him in Than'oorii. I don't think he's reasoned beyond that."

"Maybe he has," the elder Swift said thoughtfully. "We're forgetting a few things about Aquilla, Tom. The population here is relatively small and widely scattered. The government is a loose confederation, and not all that well organized. Doesn't have to be."

"Exactly!" Tom added. "K'artar know's what he's doing. He doesn't have to control all of Aquilla. All he has to do is cut off communications between Than'oorii and the rest of the world until this business is over, and all the bad guys from Earth have conveniently vanished."

Tom's father nodded. "Yes. And by the time the *Daniel Boone* figures out something's happened down here, it'll be all over. The story K'artar puts out will be so garbled no one will ever learn the truth. Relations between the star worlds and the inner planets will fall apart. We won't get back together for years—"

"B'teia." Tom faced the Aquillan girl. "How did you get here? Could you take us off the island, down to the lower portion of the city?"

"No, it's much too dangerous." Her eyes widened in alarm. "And there's no place to go, Tom. K'artar has the city well guarded!"

"I wasn't thinking about all of us," Tom said. "Just you and me. We wouldn't attract that much attention."

"What do you have in mind?" his father asked.

"There's a small research station called Lha'ii not too far from here. I'm sure they have some kind of communication gear. Something strong enough to reach at least the nearest island chain. And a message from that chain could be relayed to the *Boone*."

"You're right." The elder Swift ran a hand over his chin. "There's a good chance K'artar hasn't bothered to cover Lha'ii. But it's a big risk, Tom. You'll have to get out of Than'oorii, first."

B'teia took a deep breath. "I will get you out of Than'oorii," she said. "I promise. But Lha'ii is too far. There is no way to reach it in time."

Tom frowned. "What's the matter with swimming?"

B'teia stared at him. "*No* one swims the oceans of Aquilla at night. It is far too dangerous!"

Tom's heart sank. "Why, B'teia?"

"The Khanirii own the seas after dark. It has always been that way."

"The—what?"

"Shaldar told me about them, the last time I was here," Tom's father put in. "They live in the sea caves during the day, don't they?"

"Yes. They are—*terrible* creatures." B'teia shuddered at the thought. "The sonics keep them away from the cities, but you risk your life to go from one place to another in the open sea. There are simply too many of them!"

"There *has* to be another way," Tom said."

"Maybe there is," B'teia said cautiously. "I don't know if it'll work. But we can try, Tom."

Tom tried to remember the route as they traveled, but after a while, he was hopelessly lost. The girl led him steadily downward through twisting tunnels of coral toward the lower portion of the city.

More than once, Tom almost got stuck. Some passageways were little more than cracks in the coral structure—wide enough for the slim Aquillan girl, but nearly impassable for his own broad shoulders. Finally, B'teia put a finger to her lips and whispered in his ear.

"This is it. We will have to take the regular corridors of the city now, until we reach the water."

She slipped by him, peered cautiously through a hole in the coral, then motioned Tom forward. He knew this was the critical part of their journey. Anyone who saw him would recognize him instantly as an off-worlder. K'artar had done a good job of spreading horror stories about the visitors from Earth. Any citizen of Than'oorii who spotted him running loose would quickly sound the alarm.

"This way," said B'teia, "and stay close behind me. We're in a maintenance tunnel now—I don't think we'll run into anyone this late, but we must be careful."

The tunnel curled steadily downward in a spiral. B'teia heard voices once and paused, but no one came near. Finally, she stopped and pointed at the dark hole in the floor.

"We should be safe for the moment. See that ladder, Tom? It leads directly into the water. When we get there, follow me closely. We can't risk using any lights."

"Where do we go after that?" he asked her.

"Not far. The sea patrol has a repair shop three levels down. "I'll borrow one of their sleds."

"Good luck!" Tom whispered.

"Oh, I'm not worried." She gave him a reassuring smile, but Tom didn't miss the concern in her eyes.

The drysuit protected him from the cold, but Tom wasn't prepared for the dark. Coming out of the passage into the sea was like dropping into a can of black paint. For a brief moment, fear clutched him and held him in its grasp. He pushed the feeling aside and clung tightly to the thin line that linked him to B'teia.

She had assured him the mysterious Khanirii couldn't penetrate the city's sonic defenses. Tom believed her, but that didn't keep him from jumping out of his skin every time some tiny sea creature brushed him in the dark.

B'teia tugged the line three times, and Tom moved up beside her. They couldn't see each other, even inches away, and didn't dare use their com units. Instead, the Aquillan girl tapped his arm in a simple signal they'd worked out before.

They moved through a broad passage to a cavern just inside the city. Dim green lights dotted the walls. A half dozen sea sleds were perched on racks out of the water. Three more bobbed in a small basin not thirty yards away.

"There." B'teia pointed. "See him? Only one guard, and he's barely awake." The girl made a face. "Hardly anyone steals things on Aquilla, Tom. This—isn't easy for me."

"It's for a good cause," he assured her. "K'artar's the one betraying your planet, B'teia. Not you."

"I know. Stay here. I think I can do this better by myself. I used to work on sea sleds, and I don't want to get one that's not in good shape. When you see the sled disappear, give me about ten seconds, then drop straight down. Okay? I'll try to be there."

"Don't worry, I'll find you," said Tom. "I don't know the way back home, remember?"

He was concerned about letting B'teia go alone, then realized she was right. The Aquillan girl disappeared like smoke under the water, making no sound at all. He didn't even see her when she surfaced by the sea sled. He knew she was there because the small machine began to vanish, a slow inch at a time.

Tom counted, then let himself sink into the water. It was an eerie feeling. There was nothing to look at, nothing to give him any sense of direction. After a moment, he began to wonder whether up was really up or the other way around. In space, at least you could focus on the stars. Here, in the black Aquillan sea . . .

Something grabbed Tom's leg. He nearly let out a yell before he realized it was B'teia. He lowered himself until he felt the sea sled around him. B'teia clicked on a dim blue instrument panel. The light was barely visible, but Tom was glad to see it.

"We're far enough away now," her voice sounded in his earstud. "I think it's safe to use the com at low power."

"Do you have any idea where we are?"

"Oh, yes. The sea sleds are easy to operate. And nav-guidance chips are available for every island chain on Aquilla. Even if you're in a strange place and don't know your way around, the scope pinpoints your position. Look."

B'teia flipped the small circular scope in Tom's direction. A computer-drawn map showed clear horizontal outlines of the nearby islands in the

Kh'lai chain, from the ocean floor to the surface.

"That's Rha'mae," explained B'teia. "And there's the city of Than'oorii. Lha'ii's that very small point right there, where the south end of the chain barely reaches the surface."

Tom studied the grid squares. "We're ten, twelve miles away?"

"Yes."

The scope moved along steadily, presenting a picture of their progress. Tom noticed that the ocean floor began to drop off to starboard. Soon it vanished from the bottom of the screen.

"B'teia, is that the Dharmaii Trench?"

"Yes, but we're not all that close, and we won't be getting much nearer than we are now. It's about—three or four miles off to the right."

Tom peered into the gloom, imagining that terrible, near bottomless abyss he'd seen during the day.

"You might as well rest your eyes." B'teia grinned. "There's not a thing to see there, Tom. At least, I hope not!"

"Just thinking," said Tom.

"About the Khanirii, right?"

"I am curious," Tom admitted. "What exactly are they? In all the time I've known K'orlii, he never mentioned them."

B'teia sighed. "I'm not surprised. Aquillans

aren't real anxious to talk about the Khanirii. Basically, they're squidlike creatures with sharp, hooked claws and suckers on their tentacles. Only there's a lot more to them than that. Our scientists say they're semi-intelligent—that they evolved along with us, only didn't get as far." She repressed a shudder. "They hate us, Tom. They really do. Not like you'd hate some other animal because it's after your food. It's more than that. As if they knew we'd won, and they'd lost."

Tom frowned. "Maybe I shouldn't have suggested this trip, B'teia. Maybe coming out here is more of a risk than we ought to take—"

B'teia shook her head. "Oh, we're pretty safe in the sled. It's protected by sonics, too." She laughed nervously. "I wouldn't dare try this if we didn't have a field. No one on Aquilla's that dumb!"

Tom suddenly squinted against the dark. "B'teia, what's that? Look. Right over there."

She glanced past him and took a quick breath. "I don't know. They're lights of some kind, only—" She looked back to the scope. "There can't be anything there. That's right on the edge of the Dharmaii Trench!"

"Maybe there can't be," Tom said tightly, "but there is. Edge over a few degrees."

"Tom . . ."

He looked at her. "Correct me if I'm wrong. If Lha'ii's right over there, aren't those lights about where we saw *SeaGlobe* today?"

B'teia gasped. "Why, you're right! I don't like this, but I guess we'd better take a look." She touched the wheel lightly and the sea sled whirred off to starboard. For a moment, the lights disappeared behind a high formation of coral. Tom held his breath until they showed themselves again. The small craft passed the barrier and pulsed into clear water. Suddenly, the lights appeared almost directly beneath them, and they were moving fast!

"B'teia," Tom shouted, "bring us around, quick!"

B'teia veered away, nearly turning the machine on its side. A luminous trail of small yellow moons sped by, like ghostly pearls on a string.

"That was a little too close," she breathed. "Tom, whatever that was, it doesn't belong out here."

Tom nodded and glanced at the scope. "Take us about thirty degrees to port. There, hold it! We're right on top of them." He leaned over the dim blue glow of the console and squeezed the twin trigger grips mounted under the panel. Instantly, two harsh beams of light flared in front of the sled. He dropped them a whole ninety degrees. The beams found their target and held it.

"We've got 'em!" Tom cried.

Frozen in the bright circles of light was a heavy utility sled dragging five cargo bays in its path. Tom caught a quick glimpse of dull, heavy metal, snaky coils of cable, and a squat, cone-shaped machine. Then, the sled and its train darted quickly back into the shadows.

"What was that?" asked B'teia. "Could you tell? All I saw was . . . *Tom, hold on!*" Suddenly, she jerked the wheel and shoved in the throttle. The small sled screamed and stood on its tail, a column of frothy water boiling out of its jets. Tom slammed against his seat as the vehicle surged rapidly through the dark.

He stared at B'teia, then at the scope. Their own sled was a fast-moving blip near the top of the screen. A small dotted line came from the larger sled below. At the head of that line were half a dozen sharp points of light. Tom felt his heart in his throat. He could amost feel the deadly heat-seeking missiles nosing quickly up behind them. . . .

Chapter Seventeen

B'teia jerked the sled hard to port, nearly wrenching Tom out of his seat. For a brief moment, he thought she might be able to lose the missiles in a dizzying pattern of loops and spirals through the darkness. Then, as if they had suddenly caught their victims' scent again, the six glowing points turned in a wide arc and surged in for the kill.

Tom risked a glance at the girl. "Any bright ideas? We can't keep this up much longer!"

"One," B'teia said grimly, her eyes narrowed into the gloom. "Just one, Tom. I won't have to tell you if it works. You'll know . . ."

She pushed the wheel all the way forward and

sent them plunging straight for the bottom. Tom saw the missiles quickly correct their course.

"It's not working." he said tightly. "Every circle just brings them in closer."

The sled shook briefly, slowed for a second, then gained speed again. B'teia stared intently at the screen and twisted them through another series of jolting stops and starts.

"Current," she said, answering Tom's curious glance. "See the different shades on the scope? I'm weaving us through warm and cold layers of water. It's the only chance we've got. The missiles may—"

A distant explosion cut off her words. Then another and another. B'teia grinned weakly. "That's three of them. They had to make nine separate temperature adjustments in about five seconds."

"We've still got three on our tail." Tom jabbed a finger at the scope. "They're close, B'teia—too close."

"Boy," B'teia groaned, "you're never happy, are you?" She slammed the sled into another tortuous curve, rising and falling through the complex layers of water. Suddenly, a bright point of light came out of nowhere and blossomed on the screen.

"Look out!" Tom shouted, bracing himself in

his seat. Two seconds later, the force of the exploding missile reached them. A great hammer of water knocked the sled on its side. It tumbled awkwardly off to the left, nosing for the bottom.

The thruster jets coughed, died, caught again, then sputtered to a stop. "Uh-oh," B'teia muttered harshly, "that's all we needed!"

She fought for control, trying desperately to right the sled's course and gain power. Out of the corner of his eye, Tom saw the last two missiles moving in fast.

"Come on, machine, please!" B'teia said under her breath. Abruptly, the engines caught hold and sent them plunging down through the water. She spotted the twin streaks of green off to starboard, twisted the craft into a loop, and dropped through a blanket of icy water. The two missiles exploded as if they'd hit a brick wall. The tiny sled creaked. There was an alarming clatter from the engines. Still, it held its course, moving steadily through the water at a near-normal speed.

B'teia leaned back, let out a breath, and glanced at the scope. "We're way off course, but we can still make Lha'ii. Just barely. *If* the guidance system holds together, and the engines don't quit."

"That big sled's still back there," Tom report-ed. "But nowhere near. If they had any more missiles, I have an idea they wouldn't think twice about using them."

"They could still radio ahead and cut us off. We're not that close to Lha'ii." Concern crossed B'teia's blue-shaded features. "Tom, what was that thing doing back there? I didn't get a good look at it, but I know it had no business where it was." She shook dark hair out of her face. "Carrying cargo around in the middle of the night over the Dharmaii Trench? It just doesn't make sense."

"You forgot firing missiles at passing sea sleds."

B'teia raised a brow. "Oh, no, I didn't!"

"I'm not sure what I saw, either," Tom said. "It wasn't just cargo. It was some kind of equipment —cable, power rigs . . . and they definitely didn't want us to get a look at it. They were ready to kill us so we couldn't tell anyone what we saw. And, they were right over the trench where we saw *SeaGlobe*. It tells us something's going on down there when everyone swears there isn't."

B'teia sighed. "But even though we saw the sled, we can't prove it had a thing to do with *SeaGlobe*. Unless someone had their scope work-ing in Than'oorii, we can't prove we were fired on, either!" Suddenly, the girl's fingers wrapped tightly around his arm. "Something's out there!" she hissed. "Look at the scope, just off our stern."

"Looks like a school of fish to me."

"It's not!" Tom caught the sharp edge of fear in B'teia's voice. "I'm an Aquillan," she went on. "I know what fish look like." She scanned the row of blue dials on the small console. "Oh, no!" she gasped, "the sonics. We've lost the sonics, Tom. The missiles knocked them out!"

Something bumped the side of the sled, hung there a moment, then clattered away. B'teia jerked the craft aside. "Tom, the lights—quick! They can't stand the lights!"

"What can't?" Tom asked. But he already knew the answer and his skin crawled. The black water was thick with writhing shapes. He caught a glimpse of hooked and suckered tentacles, color-less flesh, and great, lidless eyes. Then, the monsters scattered before the sled, fleeing from the light.

"*Khanirii!*" B'teia said hoarsely. "They know the sonics are out!"

"The lights won't keep them away?"

"Not for long. They're clever. They'll come in from behind." She swallowed hard. "We've found sleds before where they knocked out the lights and . . ."

As B'teia spoke, the ugly sea creatures

swarmed in upon them from both sides. A tentacle thrashed through the open cockpit. B'teia screamed. Tom saw a great hook rip water past his chest. He lashed out at it with his knife and the rubbery limb jerked back.

B'teia turned the craft on its side and gave it all the power she could muster. Loud, metallic sounds rattled against the hull.

"What are they doing?" Tom shouted above the din.

"Banging chunks of coral against the hull! Tom, the *lights*!"

B'teia swerved the sea sled to starboard, a second too late. First one bright spot and then the other shattered and winked out. Slick, icy flesh slid over Tom's face. Something tightened like iron around his chest. He shouted at B'teia, then realized to his horror that he wasn't seated beside her any more. The creatures had ripped his safety belt away and yanked him out of the sled, which tumbled off crazily into the depths.

"B'teia!"

The Khanirii swarmed over Tom, jerked him roughly about, and squeezed him in a dozen circling coils. He cried out and struggled for air. Only the pressure of his drysuit kept him alive. The things jabbed at him blindly and pulled him toward the bottom. He stabbed out with the short utility blade. Something snatched it from his hand and flung it away.

Suddenly, a searing white light stabbed through the gloom. Tom felt the low hum of sonics in his earstud. The sound whined up the scale and out of his range. He blinked, squinted, then saw that the ugly creatures had vanished.

A yellow slit of light appeared to his right. It grew wider and became an open lock. Hands reached out and pulled Tom roughly inside. The lock closed. Pressure emptied the chamber, and in a moment Tom was breathing fresh air. Two silent figures helped him to his feet and tossed him through a small entry at the end of the lock. Tom tripped and sprawled to the floor.

A heavyset Aquillan leaned over his shoulder. "Well, Swift. Just can't mind your own affairs for long, can you?"

Tom pulled himself up. "K'artar? I guess I shouldn't be surprised to see *you* here."

"Now what kind of talk is that? After I just saved you from a terrible fate?"

Tom suddenly came to his senses. *"B'teia!* The Khanirii pulled the sled down—we've got to find her fast!"

K'artar sighed and studied his hands. "I fear there's not a thing we can do. I saw her on the scope. She headed straight for the Dharmaii Trench."

"You mean you won't even *try*?" In a rage, Tom threw himself at the Aquillan. Blue-skinned arms jerked him back and wrapped strong metal cord around his wrists.

"Swift, please." K'artar held up a hand. "I'm sorry about the girl, but I don't intend to take this craft into the trench."

"That makes sense," Tom said tightly, straining against his bonds. "You try to blow someone up with a missile, then risk your neck to save 'em. What did you pick me up for?"

"I have my reasons. And remember, you're responsible for B'teia's death. You and your meddlesome friends who schemed to steal our planet!"

"That's a lie and you know it."

"Forget it. What an off-worlder thinks doesn't mean a thing here. Not anymore."

Tom was suddenly aware of another person in the small cabin of the sled. He was hidden in the shadows, far to K'artar's right. It seemed as if he was heavily cloaked and hooded.

"That's not quite true, is it?" Tom said boldly. "I know for a fact that some off-worlders are more than welcome on Aquilla. How about *that* one, for instance? Which is he, K'artar—your partner or your boss?"

His words struck home. The hooded man

stirred and shrank back. K'artar sat up straight, his golden eyes blazing.

"It simply doesn't matter what you think," he snapped. "In a few short hours, it will make no difference who or what you may have seen down here. *No difference at all . . .*"

A blood-red sun was just rising over the horizon, turning the ocean to molten iron. K'artar's guards marched Tom up the beach to his quarters, and tossed him back in the room he'd left many hours before.

"Tom!" His father ran to him and grasped him by the shoulder. "Son—are you all right? We thought—" His grin suddenly faded. "B'teia. Where is she?"

Ben and Anita hurried in from the other room. They stopped cold when they saw Tom's face.

"She's . . . dead," Tom said flatly. "I don't see how she could have made it."

"Oh, no, Tom!" Anita shook her head and stared. "No, she can't be!"

"I'm afraid so. There wasn't anything I could do. K'artar might have saved her, but he wasn't about to." Tom quickly filled them in on everything that had happened since he and the Aquillan girl had slipped through the coral passages down to the undersea sectors of Than'oorii. When he was finished, the elder Swift walked stiffly to the window.

Then he turned and faced the others. "Tom, you should know that K'artar's men got us all up about two hours ago. Ben, Anita, myself—and Overmann and Greylock. They told us arrangements had been made to bring down the shuttle. Supposedly, we're to be taken back to the *Boone*."

Tom laughed shortly. "Not a chance. They never intended to let us go. K'artar practically told me so!"

"You didn't recognize the other person in the sled, did you?" Ben asked. "He didn't say anything, all the time you were there?"

"Nothing. He's not an Aquillan, though. I'd bet my last dollar on that. He has to be the man who's running this show. B'teia and I caught them down in the trench. They were up to something, and it's tied in with *SeaGlobe*."

"We won't see K'orlii or his family again," Ben said dully. "You know they're not about to let us get together."

"I don't want to see K'orlii," said Anita. "I couldn't tell him about B'teia."

"They're all somewhere around here," said Tom's father. "I don't think they were taken off the island. Too risky. And you're right, Ben.

K'artar's bunch wouldn't let us close to Shaldar, or any members of the Twelve Seas Council. They'll want to keep the councilors alive to back up their story—whatever that turns out to be. They'll do away with Shaldar, I'm afraid. But the others . . ." The elder Swift stalked across the room, hands jammed in his pockets. "If there was only some way we could reach Shaldar's clan. I'm sure they don't have the slightest idea what's happened to him. If they did—"

Suddenly, the door burst open and four armed Aquillans rushed into the room. "All right," snapped the leader, "everybody out. Now!" He swept the room with a short-barreled sonic rifle. Mr. Swift stepped toward the door. Tom quickly signaled Ben and Anita. The pair moved close together. Tom stepped behind them and backed up to the low table by the bed and pocketed a flat piece of metal and a small plastic box.

"You—" The guard's eyes narrowed, and the ugly snout of his weapon leveled on Tom's chest. "What do you think you're doing back there!"

"Nothing." Tom raised his hands and forced a smile. "I just don't like to go first. That's all."

The guard scowled while Tom joined the others. They were led to a low courtyard outside. The sun was a white-hot ball, setting the coral island aflame. A dozen Aquillans were mounted on Salamandaris at the far end of the courtyard. They watched the prisoners in silence, weapons ready.

The guard behind Tom jabbed him in the back with his rifle. "Go on," he said harshly, "pick out a mount and be quick about it. We want you Earthies off Aquilla before the sun goes down!"

Tom slung his legs over one of the yellow beasts. He picked up the guide cords and squinted at the bright sky. Earth was up there somewhere, a long way off. And he knew very well that K'artar never intended to let them get there.

Chapter Eighteen

Suddenly, K'artar himself urged his big Salamandari into the courtyard.

Tom's father headed straight for the heavyset Aquillan. Blue-skinned guards jerked up their weapons and warned him back, but the elder Swift ignored them. K'artar raised a hand to his followers and gave Mr. Swift an amused smile.

"Let him come," he said. "I have no fear of our—ah—esteemed visitors from Earth."

"Where are the others?" Tom's father demanded. "Councilors Overmann and Greylock? What have you done with them?"

"Why, they'll be along," K'artar replied smoothly. He glanced about the courtyard. "I'm afraid your presence here has greatly angered the people of Than'oorii. To assure your safe departure, Mordan has ordered me to split your party into two groups. We'll create less attention that way. Don't worry. You'll see the others at the shuttle."

"And where *is* the honorable Councilor Mordan this morning? I don't see him here."

"He has—other duties. They don't concern you."

"Ha!" Mr. Swift's eyes narrowed. "No stomach for the executions. Is that it?"

K'artar went rigid atop his mount. "I think you had better get back with the others. Now!"

"K'artar," Tom's father said tightly, "let's not play games with each other. I know what you have in mind for us. I'm asking you to reconsider the course you're taking. For the sake of your world and mine. This business won't end here. Can't you see that?"

K'artar's golden eyes blazed. "Oh, but it will, Mister Swift. I assure you it will!" Jerking the cords of his mount, he swerved about and shouted at his guards. "Get them out of here, you fools! We've wasted enough time as it is!"

Tom brought his Salamandari up close to his father. "He's not even bothering to pretend any more, is he?"

"No." The elder Swift scowled. "But it's not over yet, you know. We won't go down without a fight."

Tom forced a grin. "We've been in worse spots before, I'm sure. I'm just trying to think of one . . ."

They had been riding for a long time. To their right, the island rose slightly to form a white coral ridge topped by the green fronds of tropical trees. To their left was the ocean. Ahead of them, a rock formation rose about seventy feet above sea level—the closest Aquilla came to having a range of mountains.

Anita moved next to Tom. "They won't wait much longer," she whispered.

Tom nodded glumly.

"I hate to get morbid," the girl went on, "but I don't like the idea of just riding happily to my own execution. We've got to do something!"

"She's right," Ben added.

"Just keep your eyes open," Tom said. "We'll get our chance."

"Do you really believe that?" Anita said narrowly.

"I have to."

"I wish we had Aristotle along," Ben said. "We could sure use his talents right now."

The ridges became steeper and the guards led their prisoners along a narrow path through a twisting maze of coral and heavy foliage.

"I don't like the looks of this place," Anita said warily.

"A bit too spooky for my taste, too," Ben put in. "It's not—"

"Ben!" Tom cut him off. "Where are the guards?"

The Aquillans that had led them up front had vanished. Ben looked over his shoulder. There were no more guards behind them, either!

"Tom!" Ben cried. "Up there!" His arm jerked toward the ridge. At the same time, Mr. Swift shouted a warning and leaped off his mount into the brush. A hooded rider had appeared on a rise. For a brief moment, he looked at the group, then pointed into the air. Loud yells rang through the coral canyon. Riders poured out of the rocks on every side. The sound of gunfire rolled through the narrow passage!

Tom jumped off his mount as coral shattered around him. He glanced over his shoulder and saw the riders coming ahead fast. A thick stand of greenery was forty yards away. Too far, he knew. They'd never reach cover before the Aquillans ran them down. He sprinted another few feet, then dove for the shallow depression.

"Go on, head for those rocks!" he shouted to his companions.

"And where do you think you're going?" Anita asked.

"Go on, Anita! I haven't time to explain!"

Ben pulled the redhead along. Tom risked a look over the edge of his hole. Two of the riders had turned away from Ben and Anita and were headed straight for him.

Tom twisted over on his back and took the small plastic box and the piece of metal out of his belt. He had thrust it there hurriedly, using Ben and Anita for cover, when the guards burst into the room to take them away. He wasn't at all certain the holoprojector would work in the open. Maybe the bright sun would burn his images into nothing. Tom cast his doubts aside. It was far too late for maybes.

From out of the corner of his eye, he saw the riders bearing down fast. He jerked open the box of cassettes, spilling half of the tiny chips in the sand. Without stopping to check, he clicked a chip into the machine, ran his finger over the coded keys atop the box, and switched on the power. Tom hoped with all his might that it was the right chip.

The Aquillans pulled their mounts to a stop, grinned at Tom in his hole, and brought up their weapons. Suddenly, they stiffened and stared over their shoulders in disbelief. One screamed, dropped his rifle, and turned the Salamandari away. The other leaped off his mount and fled on foot.

Tom peered over the top of his depression. Across the white sand, the peaceful coral ridge had suddenly shattered in a thousand pieces. Thunder trembled over the skies. Trees shook out of their roots, and enormous stone boulders tumbled down the ridge. Salamandaris shrieked and threw their riders. Blue-skinned guardsmen stared in horror at the crushing wall of stone and ran out of the canyon.

Tom stood up. He spotted the hooded mystery man less than sixty yards away. The dark figure gripped the guide cords of his mount, stood his ground, and shouted at the retreating Aquillans.

Tom grabbed a riderless Salamandari, pulled himself atop its back, and headed for the man in black. The rider saw him, and galloped toward the trees. He looked over his shoulder and snapped off a shot from his pistol. The bullet whistled past Tom's head.

Tom's Salamandari was incredibly fast. It picked up the urgency of its young rider and stretched its taloned legs over the sand. The hooded man kicked his mount in desperation. Tom, though, was already upon him. He leaped for his black-cloaked enemy and sent him sprawling into the sand.

The man yelled, jumped to his feet, and swung at Tom. Tom ducked under the blow and came up fast with his left. The man grunted, stepped back awkwardly, and sat down hard. Tom leaned over him and jerked back the dark hood.

Henry Greylock gave him a fierce scowl!

"I'm not through with you," he raged, "not by a long shot, Swift!"

Tom grinned. "It looks to me like you are, Councilor."

Tom heard a sharp intake of breath over his shoulder. "Henry!" The elder Swift stared in disbelief. "I—can't believe you're mixed up in this!"

"Believe what you like!" Greylock barked.

Mr. Swift's face hardened. "You have a great deal to answer for—on this world, and back in the inner planets."

Tom was suddenly aware that the thundering illusion of crashing rock and stone had stopped. Over his father's shoulder, he saw Anita and Ben running toward him. Ben clutched the holoprojector in his fist, and Tom could see his broad smile a good fifty yards away. Behind Ben, stalked the familiar figure of Marcus Overmann, his face a mask of anger.

Overmann walked up and stared at Greylock.

"I hope they lock you up!" he stormed. Then he turned to Tom's father. "I don't like you, Swift. Never have. And I'm not much good at apologies. But I guess I owe you one this time." He turned and glared at Greylock. "You—you *used* me," he said tightly. "You told me one lie after another!"

"And you believed every one, you old fool!" Greylock laughed harshly. "I never could have done it without you, Marcus."

Overmann turned a bright shade of crimson and balled up his fists. Tom stepped quickly between him and the black-cloaked councilor.

"I'm afraid he used you a lot more than you know, sir. And all the rest of us, too."

Overmann frowned. "What do you mean by that?"

Tom didn't answer. Instead, he moved quickly to Henry Greylock, grabbed a handful of the man's cheek, and jerked it hard. Greylock howled in pain. Tom's hand came away with a false mustache and a ragged hunk of plasti-flesh. Abruptly, Henry Greylock was gone. The dark, piercing eyes of an old enemy blazed up at Tom.

"*Luna!*" gasped Overmann. "D—David Luna. It can't be!"

Luna grinned wickedly, then flicked his gaze around the stunned circle. "I fooled every one of you. Especially Overmann, the idiot. President of

Luna Corporation, indeed." Luna made a face. "He couldn't run a—a popcorn stand!"

A low moan started in Overmann's throat. Again, the elder Swift stepped in quickly to keep him away from David Luna.

"Now it all makes sense," Tom said. "The whole business had the David Luna trademark stamped all over it. We could never figure out who else could possibly have the money or the organization to mount these attacks."

"Somehow, you survived after your fight with the Sansoth," Ben said to Luna. "Then, I expect you used the vast funds you squirreled away from the old Luna Corporation to create a business empire for the nonexistent Henry Greylock."

"But what did you expect to gain from all this?" Mr. Swift inquired.

"I think I know," said Tom. "After Swift Enterprises and the new Luna Corporation both get kicked off the star worlds, who steps in to pick up the pieces? Henry Greylock, who suddenly has good friends like K'artar waiting to do business." Tom let out a breath. "I know you had a lot of people hired to do your dirty work, Luna— including a few misguided Aquillans who ran around in hooded outfits just like you did on occasion."

Overmann shook a fist in Luna's face. "You've

yet to answer for *SeaGlobe*. If anything's happened to that . . ."

"Find it." Luna grinned. "It's probably about sixty-thousand feet deep by now, at the bottom of the Dharmaii Trench. Crushed to the size of an egg."

"No," Tom said flatly, "it's not." He turned to his father. "*SeaGlobe*'s appearance is like a lot of Luna's clues. Fake message cubes, Aquillan rings . . . We were meant to see *SeaGlobe* down there. It was David Luna's final play to turn Aquilla's Twelve Seas Council against the inner planets. Only it wasn't really *SeaGlobe* at all, was it, Mister Luna? The equipment B'teia and I caught you and K'artar removing from the rim of the trench was part of a very imagintive set you created to give the illusion of *SeaGlobe*."

"And when Tom and B'teia got too close," put in Anita, "you set those sharks on them!"

"That was not my doing!" snapped Luna.

"It would have been, though, if you'd thought of it," Ben said drily.

"Then, what have you done with *SeaGlobe*?" Tom's father demanded.

"Like I say," Luna said sardonically, "find it, Swift!"

"We will," said Tom. "I expect it's safely hidden away at one of your old secret bases in the asteroid belt." Luna's eyes widened slightly, and Tom knew he'd come close to the answer.

"Tom, look!" Anita cried suddenly. "I—can't believe it!"

Tom turned, shouted and raced across the sand. Shaldar came toward them through the coral ridges. Armed Aquillans bearing his house sign rode behind him. Two figures leaped off Salamandaris and ran to meet Tom. The first was K'orlii, and the second was B'teia!

B'teia leaped at Tom and wrapped her arms tightly around his neck.

He looked at her, stunned. "B'teia—I thought you were dead!"

"And I thought you were!" The girl laughed. "I ran into a *very* large Throo'n down there, Tom. I think it was the grandaddy of the one we saw yesterday. It nearly swallowed me, the sea sled, *and* the Khanirii. But finally, I got that engine going and took off for Lha'ii!"

K'orlii glanced over his shoulder. "B'teia alerted my father's clan as soon as she reached the research station. Sorry we didn't get here sooner."

"Did you catch K'artar and the others?" Ben asked.

"Oh, yes," K'orlii replied. "We ran into the whole bunch scampering like crazy down the beach. Yelling something about quakes. What's that all about?"

Tom laughed. "Just a little make-believe fun. Tell you about it later."

"Well," Ben sighed, "now that David Luna's out of the way, we can get things moving again. There's still Arborea to visit, and the rest of the star worlds."

"And we've got to find *SeaGlobe*," Anita reminded him. "I doubt if David Luna will tell us where he hid it."

"Wait a minute." Tom raised his hands in protest. "If you two want to start back to work now, go right ahead. *I* intend to get in a couple of quiet days on Aquilla's beaches. Just the sea and the sand and the sun for a change. Without a bunch of Throo'n, sharks, or sea monsters cluttering up the landscape!"

Tom didn't realize that he'd soon look back on those tropical beaches with great longing. In a few short weeks, he and his friends would be embroiled in one of the most incredible adventures they'd ever experienced in *Tom Swift: The Crater of Mystery*.